SCAR ISLAND

SCAR ISLAND

DAN GEMEINHART

SCHOLASTIC PRESS /
NEW YORK

For all the librarians, teachers, and parents who
dedicate themselves to getting books into the
hands and hearts of our children.
Heroes, one and all.
—Dan

All rights reserved. Published by Scholastic Press, an imprint of Scholastic Inc., *Publishers since 1920*. SCHOLASTIC, SCHOLASTIC PRESS, and associated logos are trademarks and/or registered trademarks of Scholastic Inc.

The publisher does not have any control over and does not assume any responsibility for author or third-party websites or their content.

Library of Congress Cataloging-in-Publication Data available

ISBN 978-1-338-05384-5

10 9 8 7 6 5 4 3 2 1   17 18 19 20 21

Printed in the U.S.A.   23
First edition, January 2017

Book design by Nina Goffi

CHAPTER ONE
A DARK PLACE INDEED

It's no fun shivering when you're wearing handcuffs.

It doesn't help to be seasick, either.

Jonathan Grisby sat hunched over in the wildly rocking boat and tried not to throw up. And he tried not to let his teeth chatter together so hard that they shattered. And he tried, at the same time, to look like he didn't care.

It wasn't easy.

The little boat rocketed off of each wave and crashed into the next with a jolt that sent shots of pain into his rear from the metal bench. His clothes were wet from the salty spray. The wind kept blowing his straight black hair into his eyes, and with his hands cuffed he couldn't brush it away. The sun was already down and every second brought more darkness.

He noticed the boat's pilot grinning at him. It wasn't a nice grin. He was missing most of his teeth, and the few that he still had were brown and crooked. Tobacco juice dribbled out from his bottom lip into his scraggly gray beard.

"Ya look scared!" the pilot shouted over the whine of the outboard motor that he steered with one hand. Jonathan just blinked and looked away.

"'Tis all right to be scared, boy." The pilot eased back on the motor, slowing the boat so that he didn't have to yell. He was still smiling, and his eyes twinkled with a mean hunger.

"I'd be scared, too, if I was goin' where you be goin'." The pilot's smile widened, showing off even more stained teeth.

Jonathan threw back his head to clear the hair from his eyes and looked out over the white-capped ocean, ignoring the leering pilot. He was sitting with his back toward the front of the boat, facing the pilot and the dock they had left minutes before. Next to the pilot sat his partner. He was young, maybe seventeen or eighteen, with a kinder face. Not much more than a kid, really.

"Aw, leave 'im alone, Cyrus," the younger man said. "There's no need to tease 'im."

"I ain't teasin', Patrick. I'm warnin'." The grizzled pilot narrowed his eyes and nodded at Jonathan as he spoke. "Wouldn't be fair to toss him to the wolves with him thinkin' he's goin' on some seaside vacation! 'Tis a dark place yer goin', boy. A dark place indeed."

Jonathan, trying to ignore the old pilot, looked at the younger man, Patrick. Patrick's eyes slid away from his own. Like he felt bad. Like maybe the old man was telling the truth.

" 'Course, ye probably knew 'twas a dark place, though, didn't ya?" Cyrus continued. "That's why yer goin' there, after all. A dark place for dark youths such as yourself. Trouble-makers. Delinquents. Criminals." He savored each word in his mouth like a salty piece of bacon.

"How old are ye, boy? Twelve? Thirteen?"

Jonathan bit his lip. He didn't want to talk to Cyrus. But

he was feeling awfully lonely, handcuffed in a boat on the way to prison.

"Something like that," he said at last, with a shrug.

Cyrus's mouth widened into a wolf's grin. "Ah, yer right in the middle, then. Criminal boys, aged ten to fourteen. That's what Slabhenge is for, idn't it? Can't imagine what dark crime ya committed to get yourself sent *here,* boy. They'll have ya meek as a lamb in no time, I'd wager, beggin' to run back to yer mama's lap."

"Leave him alone, Cyrus." Patrick spoke again. "There's no point in taunting him so."

Cyrus's eyes widened innocently. "I ain't trying to taunt him, Patrick! I just feel the boy should know what he's gettin' into, is all."

Patrick frowned and looked out over the water.

"Ah, and there she is!" Cyrus crowed. "Go ahead, boy, turn around and take a look at yer new home!"

Jonathan twisted in his seat and craned his neck to get his first view of the Slabhenge Reformatory School for Troubled Boys over the rusted bow of the boat.

It was a hulking, jagged building of gray stone, surrounded on all sides by the foaming sea. The walls were high, rising up two or three stories from the crashing waves. Several towers stabbed up even higher into the gathering black clouds from each corner of the building. Each was flat-topped and crowned with a black iron railing. A few dark windows dotted the higher parts of the walls. Instead of glass, they all had thick metal bars. In a movie, it would be where the evil lord lived. Or where the good guy died.

There was no beach, no land, not even any rocks . . . The waves smashed and churned right up against the great square stone blocks of the walls. Jonathan gulped. It was worse than he'd heard—and what he'd heard had been terrible. He ground his teeth together and let the stiff ocean wind dry his angry tears before they could fall from his eyes. His hands, shackled together behind his back, squeezed into fists, then went loose.

"Pretty, ain't it?" Cyrus chuckled. His laugh turned into a cough and finished with a thick spit over the side of the boat. "It weren't always a school, ya know. 'Twas built first fer lunatics and madmen." Cyrus laughed again. "That there, for the first hundred or so years of its miserable existence, was an asylum. A madhouse. A prison fer the criminally insane."

Jonathan's eyes wandered over the moss-covered walls, the bars, the turrets and shadows. It didn't look like the kind of place where the sun would ever shine. Thunder rumbled in the dark clouds above them. He swallowed a salty ball of fear.

"Still is, I s'pose," Cyrus went on. "Only now, the psychos is just younger, is all." He finished with another throaty cackle.

He slowed the motor even more, dragging the ride out as long as he could. They were crawling now toward the stone prison, riding up and sliding down the green-black waves instead of bouncing along their tops.

"I wouldn't be thinking of escape, either, boy. Never been done. That's half a mile of ocean we be crossing, chocked with currents and undertows. Plenty of the crazies tried, of course. Threw themselves from the top of them walls there. But the sea is hungry here. It swallowed them all, without a trace. After it dashed their brains 'gainst those walls, of course. Aye, 'tis hungry water 'round here. You can feel it, can'tcha?" Cyrus was almost whispering now, his voice a hissy growl, like a bully telling a ghost story. "Why, it's eating at Slabhenge itself! See it there, chewing on them walls! Eating away at 'em, wave after wave! Did you know there used to be rocks 'round it? There did! And a pier! And a wee little sandy beach all the way around! But the sea, she's been nibbling away nigh on a century and a half. And she'll have it all 'fore she's through."

Cyrus punctuated his words with a good-riddance spit into the ocean. Then he cocked a smirking eyebrow at Jonathan. "You got yerself a cozy new home indeed, boy. A nuthouse full of delinquents, being swallowed by the sea. Ha! But don't you worry . . . if you get homesick, there's always the rats to keep you company!" Cyrus threw back his head and hollered out a laugh.

Jonathan looked to Patrick, who shrugged apologetically. "Yeah," he said. "There be plenty of rats."

They were right in the shadow of the massive walls now. The waves splashing against them were loud. He looked up to the top. There were stones missing, tumbled down into the ocean. The place was falling apart. They passed a window, two stories up. It was black and barred and shaped like a tombstone. For a moment, Jonathan was sure he saw a pale face looking out at him. He had to catch himself when the boat was rocked by a wave, and when he looked back, the face was gone. He shivered again, only partly because of the cold.

"And here we be," Cyrus said. He steered the boat up toward a darkened doorway in the wall, the same tombstone shape as the window. A heavy metal gate blocked the entry and, behind it, a huge wooden door. Stone stairs led down from the gate and disappeared into the black water.

The boat nudged up against the submerged stairs and Patrick leapt out onto the steps, a rope in his hands. He tied the boat off to a rusty metal ring jutting out from the prison wall.

"Enjoy yer stay!" Cyrus hollered as Patrick helped Jonathan step out of the boat.

"Don't let Cyrus scare ya," Patrick whispered as they climbed the steps toward the door. "Just stay quiet and keep on the Admiral's good side. Ya'll be fine."

"What makes you think I'm scared?"

Patrick looked at Jonathan with raised eyebrows, then up at the dark prison they were entering. "Well, good lord, ain't ya?"

Jonathan almost smiled. Almost. He looked up at the grim, crumbling walls of his new home. It looked bad. Just as bad as he deserved.

The wooden door creaked open. A giant stood in the doorway, wearing a dark blue uniform with shiny silver buttons. He was skinny as a skeleton but taller than any man Jonathan had seen in real life. His skin was pale, his black hair short, and he had great dark circles under his eyes. Other than one slow blink, nothing on the man's face moved.

"Is this the Jonathan Grisby?" the man asked in a deep, scratchy voice.

"Aye," Patrick answered. " 'Tis." He pulled some papers out of his jacket pocket and handed them through the bars.

"How are you, Mr. Vander?" Patrick asked. His voice cracked nervously.

The man only looked at Patrick from under his dark eyebrows, then jangled a huge ring of keys and unlocked the gate. He swung it open just far enough for Jonathan to slip through. Patrick gave his elbow one last squeeze before letting go. The gate clanged shut.

Jonathan felt himself pulled a few steps forward into darkness. The door began closing behind him with a loud creak.

"Good-b—" Patrick started to say, before his voice was cut off by the slamming of the massive door.

A huge hand, hard and strong as iron, closed on Jonathan's shoulder just as the world turned black.

CHAPTER TWO
THE SINNER'S SORROW

The pain was burning up from Jonathan's knees like hot-white fire. Sweat crawled down his back and he bit his tongue to keep from crying out.

He was kneeling on a dark wood contraption in the Admiral's office, facing the Admiral's desk. He'd been ordered to kneel there as soon as he was ushered in, and the Admiral hadn't looked up from the papers on his desk since.

The Admiral's office smelled of waxy candles, sweat, chocolate, and a vague whiff of alcohol. It wasn't a pleasant mix, and combined with the heat of the room and the sharp ache in his knees, it was enough to make Jonathan want to throw up. His shoulders were burning from being twisted back into the handcuffs after he'd changed into a drab uniform, and his stomach clenched with hunger. He'd gone from shivering in the boat to sweating in the stuffy heat of the Admiral's office. The one-piece gray garment he'd been given was stained and threadbare, and it stretched from his neck to his ankles like a prison uniform. He blew his hair out of his eyes and tried to keep his arms from going numb.

The Admiral sat behind a huge desk made of dark, shiny wood. His thin hair was mostly gray and was slicked down across his head with some kind of oily grease. His nose was the size and shape of an eagle's beak, and above were two shiny eyes, black as olives, that looked too small for the rest of his face. His eyebrows looked like two monstrous, bushy cockroaches crouched on his forehead. A patchy shadow of stubbly whiskers grew on his cheeks and chin. He was wearing a dark blue uniform jacket with fancy brass buttons, like they wore in the navy. It might have fit him when he was younger, but now his neck fat squeezed over the top button of the collar, and his belly bulged out from under the bottom three buttons, which were undone. He sat shuffling through some papers, sipping from a glass of brown liquid, and stuffing chocolates into his mouth. A crinkly pile of shiny gold wrappers grew by his elbow with each chocolate he devoured.

A blond-haired boy, a little older than Jonathan and kind of chubby, stood in the corner with his hands crossed in front of him. He was watching the Admiral with eager eyes, and from time to time shot a smug smirk Jonathan's way. He looked like a teacher's pet, but the kind that bites.

The only light came from ten or eleven tall white candles, flickering here and there from brass holders around the room.

"Brandy," the Admiral said at last. His voice was deep and breathy. Like a dragon's.

The boy in the corner sprang forward. He pulled a bottle from a shelf and poured another splash of brown liquid into the Admiral's glass. The Admiral didn't move except to exhale and raise one of his cockroach eyebrows. The kid frantically reopened the bottle and sloshed more brandy into the glass. The Admiral scowled and smacked his lips but picked up the glass and took a loud, slurping sip. The kid returned the bottle to the shelf and scurried back to his corner.

"Jonathan Grisby," the Admiral finally said. He said Jonathan's name the way most people might say the word *diarrhea*.

Jonathan swallowed.

"Yeah."

The Admiral's glass froze halfway to his mouth. His eyes slid to the kid in the corner, then back to Jonathan. The kid practically ran over to Jonathan, then leaned down to hiss into his ear.

"You gotta call him sir or Admiral, dummy!"

"What?"

"Sir! Call him sir!"

The kid retreated back to his corner, and the Admiral set down his glass.

"Jonathan Grisby," he said again. The whole room seemed to wait.

"Yes," Jonathan replied. Then, "Sir."

The Admiral smiled with half his mouth. He tapped the papers with his finger.

"This is a terrible crime you've committed, Jonathan Grisby."

Jonathan didn't answer.

"I suppose you, like most criminals, insist you are innocent?"

"No," Jonathan replied quietly, his eyes downcast. "I did it. Sir."

"Hmmm. I see. Unapologetic. Unashamed. No lesson learned yet, then?" The Admiral's face twisted into another half smile. "It will be learned, though. It will. We have wonderful ways of teaching you lessons." He took another wet sip of his brandy and swished the alcohol around in his mouth.

Jonathan swallowed a dry breath. He felt a warm bead of sweat start down his forehead.

With a grunting sigh, the Admiral rose to his feet and slumped around the desk to where Jonathan knelt in misery.

"Take, for example, the ingenious piece of furniture you're currently enjoying. Are you comfortable?"

"No, sir."

"Of course you're not," the Admiral spat. "And nor do you deserve to be." He caressed the age-polished wood with chocolate-stained fingers. "This device is known as the Sinner's Sorrow. She was here even before myself, a lovely leftover from one of Slabhenge's former lives." The Sinner's Sorrow was made all of wood, and rose as high as the Admiral's bulging belly. At its base was a rail where Jonathan's knees rested, a long piece of stained wood that was sharpened to a vicious edge that was biting at his flesh like a dull saw blade. At its top was a slanted, flat desktop and an old inkwell. "Who knows how many lunatics and criminals have knelt here, paying the price for their evil." The Admiral's eyes, blurry from liquor, lapped hungrily at the wretched wood of the Sinner's Sorrow. His gray tongue licked at his dry lips. "How does that rail feel on your young knees? It burns, doesn't it?"

Jonathan looked up, straight into the Admiral's eyes for the first time. "No," he answered in a level voice. "It doesn't burn, sir. It just hurts."

The Admiral raised an eyebrow and sniffed. "Yes, well, *you* would know, wouldn't you, Jonathan Grisby?" Jonathan looked down quickly, stung by the man's words. The Admiral cleared his throat and took a step back. "You're just the latest degenerate to feel her bite. And she is just one of the tools we use at Slabhenge to educate and civilize and correct. And you will be corrected. A crime as wicked as yours will require quite severe correction." The Admiral leaned close so that Jonathan could feel as well as hear his next words in his ear. "You *have* done terrible things, haven't you, Jonathan Grisby?"

Jonathan lowered his head and didn't answer. The Admiral wheezed out a phlegmy sigh and took a step back.

"But all that begins tomorrow. You'll see. You've arrived late. It's nearly all-dark time. Only one little thing remains to be done."

He reached for something from his desk and slid it onto the Sinner's Sorrow's little writing surface: a pen, and a blank piece of paper.

"At Slabhenge, all of our boys write a letter home to Mommy and Daddy every day. To let them know that you are safe and sound and that their investment is paying off. The mail goes out in the morning, and yours is the last letter we need."

"What do you want me to say?"

The Admiral's eyebrows dropped. The corner kid shuffled over and squeezed the back of Jonathan's arm in a hard, vicious pinch. "*Sir!*" he spat into Jonathan's ear.

Jonathan tried to shift from knee to knee to ease the growing pain.

"What do you want me to say, *sir?*"

The Admiral turned his hands palm up and spread his fingers.

"Whatever you like."

Jonathan frowned at the paper and thought of all the things he'd like to say to his parents.

"I can't write with my hands cuffed, sir."

"Of course not." The Admiral tossed a heavy ring of keys to the chubby kid, who jangled and fumbled behind Jonathan until there was a click and Jonathan felt his hands finally swing free. He rubbed his sore wrists and wiggled his stiff shoulder sockets. With a quick glance at the Admiral, he picked up the pen and scribbled out a few sentences, then folded the paper and handed it to him.

The Admiral unfolded the paper.

"*Dear Mom and Dad,*" he read aloud. "*This place is just as*

terrible as I deserve. Give my love to Sophia. Jonathan. Hmm."
The Admiral shook his head and clicked his tongue. "No,
no, this won't do. Try it again, Jonathan Grisby. You can say
whatever you wish, of course, but you cannot speak poorly of
our fine institution. We don't want them regretting the difficult decision they made to send you here. So, again, without
the parts about Slabhenge." The Admiral slid another blank
piece of paper across the desk.

"My parents didn't send me here. Sir." Jonathan knew
that it wouldn't help him at all to argue, but he felt he had to
say it. "A judge did."

The room hung in taut silence.

"Do you think I don't know that?" the Admiral asked,
and his voice was darkly low and quiet. Jonathan didn't
answer. "Yes. A judge sentenced you to a reformatory for
your heinous crime. But he gave your parents several choices,
did he not? And they chose Slabhenge, did they not?"

Jonathan swallowed. All of his trembling parts screamed
at him to let it go. But he couldn't.

"Yes, sir. But . . . only because it was the cheapest. They
had to . . . to pay for half, and we don't have—"

"Enough!" the Admiral interrupted. He bent down low
so Jonathan could look into his shiny, bloodshot eyes.
"Everything that I wish or need to know about you and your
pathetic life, I have already read. You are here because they
sent you. And, yes, we save money at the same time that we
save souls here at Slabhenge—even souls not worth saving.

Since I now know how very frugal you are, I shall make extra certain that we don't waste a single unnecessary dime on your care, other than the discipline required to correct your corrupted character. Now, the letter!"

Jonathan resisted the urge to wipe the spittle off his face that had flown there from the Admiral's mouth. He blinked down at the paper through the sweat that was dripping into his eyes. His knees throbbed. He scrawled another message and handed it to the Admiral.

"No," the Admiral said after reading it. All the teasing was gone from his voice. "Longer. More pleasant. And mention our food."

"What food, sir?"

"Our delicious and nourishing food."

"But I haven't had any food, sir. And I'm starving." Jonathan's stomach growled as he spoke.

The Admiral ground his teeth and blinked his eyes slowly. "Write the letter, Jonathan Grisby. Then dinner."

It took Jonathan seven tries to write a letter that the Admiral would accept. By the time he was done, his stomach was rumbling loud enough for all three of them to hear, and the boy in the corner was glaring at him with open hatred. The Admiral had gone through three more gold-wrapped chocolates.

"There," the Admiral said, folding up the final letter and slipping it into an envelope. "It shouldn't have been that hard. Awful things happen to boys with awful attitudes."

Too late, Jonathan wanted to answer, but he bit his lip and kept his eyes on the cracks between the stone blocks of the floor. His hair dangled down in front of his eyes and he let it stay.

"Brandy," the Admiral said, and Jonathan heard the kid hurry to fill his glass. The Admiral walked to the door and opened it.

"Mr. Warwick. Show Jonathan Grisby to his quarters."

"Yes, sir, straight away."

Jonathan's head shot up.

"What about my dinner?"

A pair of rough hands pulled him up from the agony of the Sinner's Sorrow and yanked him toward the door. The Admiral yawned as Jonathan was paraded past. He held out his hand to stop them, his fingers pressing into Jonathan's chest. He smacked his lips and leaned down to speak into his face. The sour mix of chocolate and liquor on his hot breath made Jonathan's stomach curl.

"Do you really think a boy who wastes six pieces of paper to write a simple letter deserves to be spoiled with food? Hmmm?" Jonathan's heart sank into his aching belly. The Admiral's eyes slithered to the man who was pushing Jonathan from behind. "No pillow for this one, Mr. Warwick. He doesn't have a brain worth cushioning."

"Yes, sir."

"I will see you in the morning, Jonathan Grisby. Do try to get some sleep. Tomorrow will be a very hard day for you."

CHAPTER THREE
THE HATCH

"Got on the Admiral's bad side, did ye? Ya idiot." Mr. Warwick hawked up a mouthful of snot from his lungs and spit it onto the floor. He was guiding Jonathan through a twisting labyrinth of dark hallways and steep, shadowy stairwells. The whole place—floor, walls, stairs, and ceiling—was made of the same huge blocks of gray stone. Their way was lit only by a hissing lantern that swung from Mr. Warwick's outstretched hand.

"Ye all do, nearly. Bunch of scum, ye are. The Admiral knows ye fer what ye are, aye." Jonathan stumbled on a slippery step and Mr. Warwick jerked him roughly back up to his feet. "Still, ye got it better'n some. You get a blanket, at least. More than ye deserve, likely."

"Lucky me," Jonathan muttered.

Mr. Warwick spit again and flicked Jonathan in the ear hard enough to make his eyes burn.

"Don't ye be gettin' smart, now. Smart gets ye nowhere good 'round here."

"Look, Mr. . . . Warwick, or whatever," Jonathan started, rubbing his ear. "Could I get something to eat, something small, even? A biscuit or an apple or something? I haven't eaten since breakfast."

Mr. Warwick scratched between his legs and snorted. "Ah, me heart's just a-breakin'. Poor little criminal's got 'im an achin' tummy!" He coughed out a mean, small laugh.

Suddenly, he pulled to a stop and grabbed Jonathan's arm. "Ah, now look here, boy." His voice was tight and breathless. He held up the lantern to show a narrow stairway leading down from the corridor they were in. The stairs curved down and around a corner before they were lost in darkness. A low rumbling, gurgling sound and the salty, rotten smell of stale seawater wafted up to where Jonathan and his guard stood. A frayed rope stretched as a flimsy gate across the stairway opening.

"Don't ye never stumble down this wretched staircase, boy," Mr. Warwick whispered. He leaned close to Jonathan's face in the yellow lantern light. For the first time, Jonathan saw his wrinkled face and his one puckered, empty eye socket. He shivered and pulled back.

"Why? What's down there?"

Mr. Warwick's lips pulled back to show a toothless smile. "Why, the Hatch, me boy! A door, of sorts. And beyond it: death and despair and darkness! It be a door that holds back a *monster*. Ancient she is, and dark, and hungry, and just barely held back. She's there, though, knockin' and waitin' and bidin' her time! Not locked in, boy, but locked *out*—and not for long, I'd wager!"

Mr. Warwick stared into Jonathan's face with his one eye for a breathless moment before breaking into a wheezing cackle. "Aye," he said, running his tongue over his toothless gums. "Death himself is yer downstairs neighbor. Yer room be straight up here, with the other no-goods."

Mr. Warwick stumbled ahead with the swinging lantern. Jonathan stood for a second longer, his eyes peering past the rope and down the darkened stairs. He knew the morbid cyclops was just trying to scare him, the new kid, with his ghost stories. And Jonathan was past believing in most kinds of monsters. But up from the stairwell came a thump and a rattle, then a slurping growl. He shivered and hurried after the retreating yellow light.

They rounded a corner and then stopped before a large metal door. At eye level, just above Jonathan's head, was a small rectangular opening crossed with metal bars. Mr. Warwick rapped on the door with his knuckles. The knocking echoed in the cold hallway. Water dripped all around them in the darkness, and there was occasional scurrying, off in the shadows.

Through the opening in the door came the sound of shuffling footsteps punctuated by the steady *thwock* of a cane hitting the stone floor. A bald forehead and a glaring pair of eyes appeared in the little barred window.

"It's I, Mr. Mongley," Mr. Warwick said to the eyes. "I've got me the new one here. No pillow for 'im, either, so you know."

The half face disappeared and there was a jangling of keys and then the door swung open. Mr. Warwick pushed Jonathan through the doorway and stepped in behind him.

Beyond the door was nothing but darkness, but Jonathan could tell from the echoes and the movement of the air that the room was large, with a tall ceiling. Besides the smell of ocean and mold and wet stone, there was also here the smell of sweat and bodies and the unmistakable odor of an over-used bathroom.

The man who must be Mr. Mongley stood glaring at him sideways, one shoulder hunched over. He shielded his eyes from the light of the lamp.

"It's all-dark," he rasped. His voice was a scratchy hiss, like his throat was stuffed with cotton. He was wearing the same blue uniform that Mr. Warwick and Mr. Vander had. Without another word he turned and limped off, thumping away into the darkness on a crooked black cane.

"Go on, go on," Mr. Warwick grunted, poking Jonathan in the spine.

Jonathan's eyes darted around the shifting shadows as he followed the hunched form of Mr. Mongley. There were puddles on the floor here, too, big and small. He could just make out, on both sides of him, openings in the walls. Large rectangular doorways, each with a lightless room behind it, each blocked with the sturdy metal gate of a jail cell. They *were* jail cells, he realized. Or, he reminded himself, *madhouse cells*. They were cells built to hold the criminally insane of the previous century.

There were no windows. No torches. Not even a single, flickering candle. There was no light at all in the room, none except the shifting, swaying light of the lantern behind him. But in that unsteady light, Jonathan saw a silent face behind each black cell door as they passed it. A pair of hands, sometimes, gripping the iron bars. The light was too dim and the room too big for him to see any of them clearly, but he knew they could all see him, walking in the lantern light. He could feel all their eyes on him.

Mr. Mongley stopped at a cell door and rattled it open with his ring of keys. He stepped to the side and Mr. Warwick started to shove Jonathan in.

"Wait," he protested. "I can't sleep in here!"

Mr. Warwick gave him a final push and slammed the metal door. "Then don't," he said through the bars as Mr. Mongley turned the key in the lock.

"What about a bathroom?"

Mr. Warwick raised the lantern and held it through the bars. The cell was narrow—Jonathan could have almost touched both walls with a hand if he stood in the middle. A few feet from the cell door, against the side wall, was a single bed on a metal frame, covered with a thin, lumpy mattress and one ragged blanket. No pillow, of course. And no window. No chair. No desk. No sink. The only thing in the cell besides the bed was a rusty bucket sitting in the back corner.

Mr. Warwick swung the lantern toward the bucket. "That there's yer night bathroom, boy. Sleep tight. And Mr. Mongley don't take to no talkin' after all-dark, so I'd be keepin' yer mouth shut tight, if I was you. Which I ain't, thank the devil."

And with that the light jerked away and disappeared step by step, leaving Jonathan to stand in thickening, choking blackness. Mr. Mongley's cane tapped away with it. There was the creak of the metal door opening, then a final crashing clang as it slammed shut, taking the last of the light with it.

At first, there was nothing but silence and absolute darkness. Jonathan could hear his own desperate breathing, and the hammering of his heart. A cold draft blew through his cell door and goose bumps popped up on his neck. He wrapped his arms around his body.

Water dripped and dropped and dabbled all around, a crazy constant pattering and pittering. And then, all around the room, he heard a scraping and shuffling sound. He strained his ears and then realized that it was all the other boys, walking back from their cell doors to crawl into their skinny beds. Mixed in was the squinchy squeak of mattress springs as bodies lay down and curled up.

He cocked his ear and stepped toward the wall to his right. There had been a watching face in the cell next door, he remembered, but he didn't think he'd heard the sound of footsteps or mattress springs from that cell yet. His closest neighbor might still be standing at his cell door, only a few feet away.

Jonathan leaned one hand against the damp stone wall and pressed his face through the bars closest to the wall.

"Hey!" he whispered, as loudly as he dared. "Is anyone there?"

There was no response.

"Hey!" he tried again.

There was a sound, like a sigh or a breath. He screwed his eyes shut in the darkness and listened harder.

"What?" Jonathan asked.

There was the sigh again, just as faint, but this time Jonathan's ears picked up the sounds inside it.

"*Quieter,*" the voice whispered, almost impossibly quiet. "*Mongley hears everything.*"

"Mongley's gone!"

"*No. He always stays. All night. Quieter.*"

Jonathan shook his head. He couldn't possibly speak any quieter.

"What kind of place is this?" he asked.

"*A bad place. Quieter.*"

A chill shook Jonathan's body. His teeth were starting to chatter. It made the whispering harder.

"It can't be as bad as it seems."

The voice paused before answering. Like it wanted to say a lot more than it could in a smoke-thin whisper.

"*No. It's worse. You'll see tomorrow,*" the voice breathed at last. "*Quieter.*"

Jonathan gulped and took a few deep, shaky breaths. Behind him was a cold bed with no pillow and a bucket he didn't even want to think about. He changed the subject.

"I'm Jonathan. What's your name?"

"*Walter.*"

"Do you have any food?" Jonathan's hunger got the better of him, and his rumbling belly grabbed him by the throat when he asked the question, raising his voice above the whisper he'd intended. His question came out as a desperate plea. It echoed, just barely, in the dark cavern of the room.

Somewhere off in the darkness, Jonathan heard a grunt. Then, coming closer through the total blackness, the tap-tap-tapping of a cane. Beside him he heard Walter scuttle back to his bed. Jonathan held tight to the metal bars, eyes wide, his head rotating from side to side, seeing nothing. The tapping came closer, and closer, straight toward him.

Finally, it stopped. In the echoing stone chamber Jonathan couldn't tell where it had stopped—in the middle of the room, or inches away. He waited, breathless.

There was a whoosh and another grunt and then Jonathan was hit by a shocking surge of freezing water. It hit him full in the face and drenched his clothes. His breath was sucked from his lungs by the frigid water.

"*No talking,*" Mr. Mongley hissed like a dying rattlesnake. Jonathan gasped and coughed, his body racked by violent shivering. "*The next bucket won't be water.*"

The cane tapped away, quieter and quieter, and then fell silent. Jonathan stood shivering, his teeth rattling. Then he turned and felt his way back to his bed.

He eased down onto the mattress. It was about as thin as a folded-up newspaper and just about as soft. He pulled the scratchy blanket around his soggy self and curled into a shaking ball.

Something snuffled and squeaked under his bed.

He blinked into blackness and tried not to imagine a day that could be any worse than the one he'd just had. He bit his lip and ran his fingers over the skin of his arms. After a few moments, his thoughts were no longer for himself or his cold or his hunger. Shivering alone in the black, his thoughts were for Sophia. And his silent tears, when at last they came, were for her, too.

JONATHAN'S FIRST LETTER HOME

Dear Mother and Father,

I have arrived at the Slabhenge Reformatory School, safe and sound. The trip was pleasant. The school is quite impressive and the food is very good. I'm better fed here than I was at home! Although I am a little angry at you for making the difficult decision to send me here, I am sure that it will all be for the best. Give my love to Sophia.

Your loving son,
Jonathan Grisby

CHAPTER FOUR
A DARK TALE, TO BE SURE

Jonathan gripped the knife in his hand and fought back the tears that burned in his eyes.

"My god," he whispered to the boy next to him. "How long do we have to do this?"

The boy looked around to make sure no adults were within earshot. The dark brown skin of his head was shaved almost bald, and it glistened with sweat from working in the hot, crowded kitchen.

"Until they tell us to stop, man," he murmured, handing Jonathan another onion.

Jonathan had opened his eyes that morning to the same nightmare he'd fallen asleep in. Freezing cold. Ravenously hungry. Lost in hopeless darkness. They'd been roused from their sleep by Mr. Mongley's hoarse whisper-shout and the clang of his cane against cell bars, then lined up and marched to a huge, cluttered kitchen. With no welcome or instruction, he'd been handed a knife and a basket of onions and shoved over to a long counter. He was three onions in now, and his belly was howling for food.

He looked around as he worked. All around him, other boys were bustling and cooking and chopping, each wearing the same dingy gray one-piece uniform that he was. There seemed to be about fifteen of them. Some looked a little older than him, some a little younger. None of them looked happy.

"Don't they have, like . . . a cook, or something?"

The kid snorted and rolled his brown eyes.

"Yeah, right. Why pay a cook when they can make our sorry butts do it? The more we do, the more money goes in the Admiral's pockets." He wiped at his eyes, then nudged Jonathan and pointed with his chin at Mr. Warwick, glaring at them from the corner. "*Quieter*," he whispered.

Jonathan smiled. "You're Walter?"

The kid nodded. "You almost got me drenched, man. Jonathan, right?"

"Yeah."

"Well, welcome to Slabhenge. How long you here for?"

"Ten weeks," Jonathan answered. It hadn't sounded that terrible in the courtroom. He'd almost *wanted* to come, to get away from . . . everything. But standing there now, ten *hours* seemed like more than he could stand.

Walter whistled and his wide eyes shot up to Jonathan.

"*Ten*? Geez, man, what did you *do*?"

Jonathan looked into Walter's eyes for just a moment, then looked away again quickly.

"Why? How long are you here for?" he asked.

Walter snorted.

"Well, I was sent here for four weeks. But that was almost two months ago."

"Why are you still here?"

Walter rolled his eyes again.

"Everyone stays longer, man. Just when you're about done with your time, the Admiral sends a little letter. To your folks, to whatever judge or state sent you here. Tells how you're coming along fine, but there's still more work to do, that he's sure you'd come right around if he had just a little more time to educate you." Walter's voice dripped with scorn. "And he offers to extend your education. At a reduced rate." He finished chopping an onion and started on the next. "You're supposed to be here for ten weeks? Sorry, man, but I bet you don't get outta here in less than fifteen."

Jonathan chopped numbly, trying to digest what he'd been told.

"How do you know all this?"

"Benny," Walter answered. He almost spat the name out. He motioned with his chin across the kitchen to a kid standing at a sink, lazily splashing a scrub brush around a soapy bowl. Jonathan recognized him—he could still feel the painful pinch the kid had given him on his arm.

"I saw him last night," Jonathan said. "He works in the Admiral's office."

"Yeah. Little punk. He tells us all about those letters he stuffs into envelopes and addresses. Just loves to tease us, you know?"

Walter looked around the kitchen, pointing out kids with his knife.

"That big black kid there is Tony. He's cool. The guy grating cheese is Jason. He's super quiet, but seems all right. Stole a car, I heard. Next to him is David. Doesn't say much, but he's tough. Do *not* call him Chinese, okay? He's Japanese. Couple of kids made that mistake early on and had black eyes to show for it."

Jonathan's eyes darted around the room, trying to keep up with Walter's fast talk and chop onions at the same time without cutting off a finger.

"See those two meatheads working together to stir the oatmeal? That's Roger and Gregory. Dumb as catfish and just about as friendly. Miguel's the one making coffee. He's funny. Or thinks he is, anyway. That tall dude manning the toaster is Francis. Total jerk. But the *real* jerk is Sebastian. Him you gotta watch out for, man. He's out setting the table, I think."

Walter looked over and saw Jonathan fumbling with his onion. "It's easier if you pull your sleeves up, man." He reached over toward Jonathan's arms. "Here, let me show—"

"No," Jonathan snapped, pulling his arms away. "I mean, no, thanks. I'm still cold. It was a wet night."

Walter looked at him, then shrugged. "Yeah. Mongley got you good. I swear that guy can see in the dark."

"You guyth need help with the onionth?"

Jonathan looked up at a new kid who'd joined them at the cutting board. Or rather, down at him. He was a good foot shorter than Jonathan. He had blond hair trimmed in a bowl cut, green eyes, and skin as pale white as paper. His chin and his nose were kind of pointy.

"Hey, Colin. This here's Jonathan. First day."

"Of courth. I heard the thplath latht night."

"The what?" Jonathan asked.

"The thplath. From the bucket. Almotht everyone geth the bucket on their firtht night."

Walter looked up at Jonathan. "Colin and I got here on the same day. He talk*th* funny." Walter exaggerated the lisp, but he gave Colin a friendly dig with his elbow when he said it.

Colin nodded. He smiled, a fleeting little smile at the corners of his mouth that flashed like a bird and then vanished, but his eyes stayed down on the onion he was cutting. "Yeth," he said quietly. "I'm thure he notithed."

"It's all right," Jonathan said quickly, his voice as soft as Colin's. "My—I have—I used to know someone who talked different, too." Colin looked up, for just a second, at Jonathan and smiled. Then his eyes dropped back down.

"Well, welcome to Thlabhenge," he said softly.

All around them, savory smells grew stronger. Sizzling onion, greasy bacon, frying eggs, boiling potatoes. Across the kitchen the chubby kid who Walter had said was named Tony was flipping golden, round pancakes on a griddle. Jonathan almost had to lean on the cutting board to not collapse.

"At least the food here is good," he said. "I'm gonna eat 'til I puke."

Colin and Walter exchanged a glance.

"Thith food ithn't for uth," Colin whispered.

"What? Who's it for?"

"*Them*," Walter answered with a meaningful look over Jonathan's shoulder. Jonathan risked a backward glance. Behind him was a long, glassless window that looked out into a big room with two long tables. Sitting at the closest table were five or six adults, including two he recognized: Mr. Vander, the tall zombie who'd met his boat, and the hunched-over form of Mr. Mongley. As he watched, the Admiral came marching in the door, still wearing his blue navy jacket. A sword hung in a scabbard on his hip. He was wearing baggy blue pants that met his shiny black boots at his knees. A huge, old-fashioned wide-brimmed hat was held under one arm, the triangular kind you see in history books, being worn by ship captains or Napoleon Bonaparte. The Admiral flopped down in a heavy wooden high-backed chair at the empty table.

"They get all this?" Jonathan asked.

Colin and Walter nodded.

"What do we get?"

"Oatmeal, usually," Walter replied.

"Thometimth toatht."

Jonathan bit his lip and nodded.

"Great."

Eventually, all the food was ready on platters and in bowls lined up on the counter by the kitchen door. Jonathan licked his lips and watched the steam rising off the hash browns, pancakes, scrambled eggs. He saw the gooey cheese oozing out of the omelets, the salty grease pooling on the platter under the bacon, the butter melting on the flaky biscuits.

"When do *we* eat?"

"*When we tell ye to!*" a voice barked in his ear. Jonathan jumped and turned to see Mr. Warwick's one eye glistening at him. "*If* we tell ye to. Now grab a bowl, boy."

One by one the boys filed by and picked up a serving dish and carried it out through the door. Jonathan grabbed a butter dish and a little pitcher of syrup and followed. The table was already full when he got there, but he found a tight spot for his items. The men were all slurping and reaching and smacking their lips, piling their plates high with food and shoveling it by the forkload into their mouths.

The boys, once the food was delivered, stood back against the stone wall with their hands behind their backs.

"More coffee," the Admiral said through a mouthful of sausage, and a boy darted back to the kitchen.

"And salt!" a bearded man with gold earrings shouted after him.

When the boy returned with the salt and coffee, the Admiral swallowed his mouthful and glowered up at the boys against the wall.

"All right," he said, wiping some grease off his chin with the back of his hand. "Go clean and eat. That kitchen better be spotless or it'll be no lunch for the lot of you!"

The boys turned and filed toward the kitchen. Jonathan followed with them but was stopped in his tracks by the Admiral's foul voice.

"Jonathan Grisby! A word with ye."

Jonathan gulped and stepped out of line and walked over to where the Admiral sat.

The Admiral stabbed a piece of roasted potato. He slid the silver blade of the knife into his mouth and leaned back to look Jonathan in the face. Jonathan waited with downcast eyes as the Admiral chewed and swallowed.

"How was yer first night, Jonathan Grisby?"

Jonathan didn't want to do or say anything that would risk his breakfast getting taken away like his dinner had the night before.

"Fine, sir."

"Can be a long night with no pillow, I imagine. Neck a bit sore, eh?"

"No, sir. I'm fine, sir."

"Mmm. Good. I read your file last night. 'Twas fine bedtime reading. The sad history of Jonathan Grisby, boy delinquent. It is a dark little tale, isn't it?"

Jonathan blinked and breathed through his nose.

"Yes, sir. I guess so."

A rotten smile spread across the Admiral's face.

"Oh, it don't take any guessin'. 'Tis a dark tale, to be sure." The Admiral leaned forward and lowered his voice. "Between you and I, a lot of these boys don't really deserve to be here. A belt and a bellow would suffice for most of them, I'd say. But you, Jonathan Grisby. You *do* deserve to be here, don't you?"

Jonathan swallowed and sniffed. He shifted from foot to foot. Then he looked up into the Admiral's obsidian eyes. And nodded.

"Yes, sir," he said, his voice a hoarse whisper. "I do."

The Admiral slurped half a sausage into his mouth and nodded. His eyes narrowed to dark reptilian slits and his smile widened. He chewed slowly, his black eyes burrowing like beetles into Jonathan's.

"I'm going to take a personal interest in your education here, Jonathan Grisby. A boy like you will require more focused attention, I believe. So troubled. So . . . *evil.* We'll begin your education right after Morning Muster today." The Admiral swallowed and then gulped a mouthful of coffee. He waved his hand dismissively at Jonathan. "That'll be all. Don't just stand there like a dead chicken."

Jonathan retreated numbly to the kitchen, where all the other boys were busy sweeping and scrubbing and cleaning up. A great cauldron bubbled on one of the stoves, and his nose sniffed hungrily at the smell of oatmeal.

Jonathan's growling belly was interrupted by a sharp shove from behind. A tall kid with scalp-short black hair glared down at him. His nose was broad and flat, like a tiger's. It was bumpy, like it had been broken before. More than once.

"What do you think you're doing?" the kid demanded. "You don't help, you don't eat."

"Oh . . . I . . . what . . ." Jonathan stammered, panicked at the thought of missing breakfast. "What do you want me to do?"

The kid scowled and looked around. He pointed at a pile of logs by the wall.

"Add more wood to the stove. It's about burned down." He bent over and opened the iron door at the bottom of the stove. A wave of heat blasted out. Jonathan looked at the glowing red coals, the licking red flames, the flickering, hungry fingers of fire.

"No," he said, shaking his head.

"What?"

"No, I—I can't. I don't like fire."

"You don't *like* fire?" the kid snorted.

"God, Sebastian, leave him alone. It's his first day." The voice came from Tony, the kid who'd been flipping pancakes. He lifted his chin in greeting at Jonathan and then grabbed a couple of logs from the pile and tossed them into the stove. He kicked the door shut with his foot and brushed past the broken-nosed kid and back to the pot he'd been scrubbing.

"Name's Tony," he shouted over his shoulder. "Welcome to Slabhenge, kid."

Sebastian scrunched his broken nose at Jonathan before turning away.

As the cleanup got done, the boys lined up behind the cauldron of oatmeal. Walter pulled Jonathan and Colin into line with him.

"This place stinks, man," Walter said. "No joke. But you'll get used to it." He smirked and cocked his eyebrows at Colin. "If short stuff here can make it, I'm sure you'll be all right."

Colin smiled back, for just a flash. He pursed his lips and pulled on one ear, his eyebrows screwed up thoughtfully. "Yeah," he said. "There'th no bookth, though. That'th the wortht part. I mith bookth."

Colin looked so small and sad and quiet, standing there pinching his own ear. He looked nothing like a hardened delinquent in need of reform.

"What did you do?" The question blurted out of Jonathan's mouth. "Why are *you* here?"

Colin ducked his head further. His eyes flitted up to Jonathan's and then back down.

"I'm a klepto," he whispered. Then he kind of giggled.

"A what?"

"A kleptomaniac. I thteal thtuff. Loth of thtuff. I can't help it."

Walter shook his head.

"Man, why don't you just say 'thief'? It's what your mouth *wants* to say."

Colin smiled, just a little bit.

"I'm a thief. A thneaky, thneaky thief." Jonathan smiled back at him. "Why are you here?"

Jonathan opened his mouth and shut it. He swallowed. Then the line started moving.

They filed past the great pot of oatmeal, where Benny stood, dolloping a ladle of the steaming gray glop into each of their bowls.

Jonathan grabbed a bowl from a pile on the counter and held it out when he got to the front of the line. Benny scooped his ladle into the pot and held it out toward Jonathan's bowl.

"No, Benny," Sebastian's voice said from behind him. "No breakfast for the new kid. He didn't do a thing to help clean up."

Jonathan spun around. "I'm *starving*, please—"

"Keep talking." Sebastian cut him off, leaning in close. "And it'll be no lunch, either."

Tears sprang to Jonathan's eyes. If there'd been anything in his stomach, he would have thrown it up.

He felt a gentle hand grab his elbow.

"Come on," Colin's voice whispered. "It'th all right."

Jonathan turned and let Colin lead him out to the tables, his heart and stomach as empty as his bowl. He sat down on the hard wooden bench between Walter and Colin. The other boys were all gulping and swallowing their oatmeal, not bothering to let it cool down. Jonathan closed his eyes and tried not to pass out.

Colin's elbow nudged him in the side. He opened his eyes. Colin had slid his bowl full of oatmeal in front of Jonathan and put Jonathan's empty bowl in front of himself.

He grinned a secret little grin at Jonathan and darted his eyes around.

"Hurry and eat it," he whispered. "Morning Muthter ith in a few minuth."

"But . . . you need to eat, too!" Jonathan hissed.

Colin shook his head and his smile stretched. He almost showed his teeth.

"It'th okay. I dethpithe oatmeal."

"Aren't you hungry?"

Colin nodded, his eyes shining. He pointed with his eyes down to his lap, and Jonathan looked down to where Colin was hiding his hands under the table. In one hand he held a biscuit slathered with jam. In the other, a glistening sausage link.

"How did you—" Jonathan started to ask.

Colin winked and took a quick bite of the biscuit.

"I'm a thneaky thief, remember?"

CHAPTER FIVE
MORNING MUSTER

It was Morning Muster time. The boys were marched outside into the drizzly gray courtyard. A light rain was falling, and bunched-up piles of clouds blackened the sky. Thunder rumbled in the not too far distance.

The boys trudged over to a line of small stone blocks on the ground, each about the size of a brick and spaced a few steps apart from one another. Without a word, each boy stepped up and squeezed his feet onto one, found his balance, and then stood at shaky attention. Jonathan took a breath and did the same.

The block was just wide enough for both his feet to fit on it, pressed tight together. The tips of his toes and the backs of his heels hung over the front and back. He wobbled and steadied himself and then looked up.

The courtyard was the size of a basketball court. He'd walked through it briefly his first day, following Mr. Vander in his handcuffs, but he'd been too tired and scared then to look close or notice much. He could see, to his right, the steep arched doorway, closed and locked, that led to the watery stairs he'd come in on. There were doorways on each wall that he could see, all closed.

The floor and walls of the courtyard were made of the same big gray blocks of stone that the rest of the building was made of. Green moss grew between the cracks in places.

The walls stretched high above them, thirty or forty feet, blocking out most of the sky and a good deal of the light. The part of the sky that was visible was getting darker and more ominous by the second. There was a flash of lightning.

The courtyard's stone block ground was flat and covered with so many big puddles that it was nearly one shallow lake. The surface of the puddles were pocked and pecked by more falling rain. Shifting snaps of wind whistled around the courtyard, chilling the boys and blowing Jonathan's hair into and out of his eyes.

The door to their left swung open, and the whole group of men from breakfast slumped out with the Admiral at the front. The ridiculous wide hat, roughly triangular, sat on his head, and the sword still swung at his side. The last two men in line came out sideways, grunting and holding the Sinner's Sorrow between them. They plocked it down with a wet thud on the stones before the boys. Jonathan looked at the kneeler's sharp, hard edge and winced.

The men formed a line facing the boys. They stood in an oily black puddle with their boots and shoulders touching. Jonathan counted them—eight adults. The Admiral stood in the center of the line, his arms at his sides and his chin held regally high.

Mr. Warwick, standing on one end of the line, held the wooden handle of a big brass bell in his hand. When the two men who'd carried the Sinner's Sorrow joined the line, he rang the bell. The dull metal clanging bounced around the grim gray walls and up to the storm-choked sky.

"Morning Muster, November the fifth!" Mr. Warwick hollered. The man on the other end of the line pulled some papers out of his coat pocket and held them with both hands in the wet wind.

"James Amherst!" he shouted.

"Here, sir. Content and well cared for, sir!" a boy Jonathan hadn't met yet shouted back.

"David Okada!"

"Here, sir. Content and well cared for, sir!"

"Benedict Fellows!"

"Here, sir," the kid called Benny answered. His voice sounded greasy even when he was shouting through a rainstorm. "Content and well cared for, sir!"

"Jonathan Grisby!"

Jonathan gulped and looked around. He almost stumbled off the block but caught himself.

"Here, sir," he called. His voice sounded thin and meek and was nearly lost in the windblown rain. "Content and well cared for, sir!"

The Admiral smirked.

"Colin Kerrigan!"

"Here, thir." Colin didn't shout—Jonathan wasn't sure he even *could* shout—but he did speak at more than a shy whisper. "Content and well cared for, thir."

All the boys were called, sixteen in all, and each gave the same answer. When they were done, the man folded the papers and slipped them back into his coat. "Sixteen charges, sir, all present and all report being content and well cared for, sir."

The Admiral grimaced and wrinkled his nose.

"Thank you, Mr. Washburn. Put it in your report."

The Admiral stepped forward. He took a few soggy steps toward the line of boys, his eyes sliding like a snake from boy to boy. He poked at something between his teeth with his tongue.

He had just opened his foul mouth to speak when the boy to Jonathan's right wobbled. The boy pinwheeled his arms to catch his balance, but it was too late and he dropped a foot off his block to the ground.

The Admiral's mouth snapped shut and he raised one of his cockroach eyebrows. He shook his head and clucked his tongue.

"To the Sorrow, Miguel Vargas."

The boy's head dropped.

"Yes, sir," he mumbled and slouched to the Sinner's Sorrow, its black wood dotted now with raindrops. He knelt on the horrible device and squinched his eyes shut. Jonathan remembered well the bite of that sharp rail. He bit his lip and looked away from Miguel.

The Admiral watched him for a moment and then looked back to the boys still on the blocks.

"Boys, we have a new student among us. As I'm sure you know. A young Jonathan Grisby, twelve years old." As he talked, the Admiral strode slowly down the line of balancing boys. He stopped before Jonathan. "Ten weeks we are supposed to have him. But for a crime of his magnitude, I think we may need him longer." Jonathan met the Admiral's sinisterly gloating eyes for a second, then looked quickly away.

The Admiral resumed walking down the line. "I thought it a good idea this morning," he said, his voice booming so as to be heard over the rising wind and growing thunder, "to remind you all what you are and why you are here. For Jonathan Grisby's benefit."

At the end of the line, a boy's foot dropped to the ground. Without a word he shook his head and walked to the Sinner's Sorrow. Miguel jumped gratefully up from the kneeler and limped stiffly back to his stone block. The new boy scowled and took his place on his knees. The Admiral waited for them each to get into place before continuing. By now he was back at the center of the line, and he took a step back so he could throw his grisly gaze over all his charges.

"Bloody, disgusting little scabs, boys," he said. He enunciated each word clearly and precisely. "That is what you are. The very scabs of civilized society." He smiled an ugly, pinched smile, then let it drop from his face. "And why, you might ask, do I call you scabs?" He started walking again, his eyes up at the clouds and the occasional, quick flickers of lightning. His voice lilted and rose like a schoolteacher's.

"Scabs, as you know, are nasty little things. An otherwise healthy body gets a wound. A disfigurement. And it begins to bleed, that wound. And it forms a dirty little scab. Good for nothing. An unhealthy nastiness. An ugliness. Well, boys, it is our civilization itself that is sick. It is too tolerant. Too soft. It is . . . *wounded*. Bleeding from its rottenness. And you, lads, are the scabs. The bad little bits that nobody wants."

He stopped and cleared his throat. Scratched at his nose. Looked at the line of boys with distaste. "And so society sends you here. Society picks you off like the little scabs that you are and flicks you out here to my island. To try and turn you into something better. And if I can't?" The Admiral lowered his chin and looked at them from under his eyebrows. "Well, at least we keep you out of the way for a while. And we give you what you deserve."

He raised his head again and trudged deliberately through them, between two boys. His elbow bumped one— not too gently—and the boy stumbled to the ground. He kicked at a puddle and took the second boy's place on the kneeler.

When the Admiral's voice bellowed again, it was moving behind them.

"So what can we do with you? Why are you all such incorrigible delinquents? It's simple." The Admiral paused dramatically. "Weakness. And rot. You've been spoiled and now you are rotten and weak and it is up to me to fix you.

So, at Slabhenge, we do not do what other schools do. We do not read stories. We do not talk about your . . . *feelings*. We do not play with numbers or write tedious essays about what you did last summer. What you did last summer was get weak and rotten. What you do here is *work*. You work. And, yes, sometimes you suffer. That, I'm afraid, is the cost of improvement. That is where strength comes from, boys."

The Admiral's voice circled slowly around until he was once again standing before them. The rain had picked up and was now a bit more than sprinkling. It dripped down Jonathan's face and off the brim of the Admiral's hat. The puddles were growing, swallowing the few blocks left between them. It was almost as dark as night, and flashes of lightning splashed the courtyard with wild shadows.

"We will work the weakness out of you!" With a flourish the Admiral yanked his sword out of its scabbard. It flashed bright silver in the dim, stormy light. "We will cut all the rottenness out of your character, if we can. We will certainly try. Just as society cut the rottenness out of itself by sending your worthless hides to Slabhenge, Slabhenge will cut the rottenness out of you. We will bleed the infection right out of you."

The Admiral took a step backward toward the line of men, his eyes still on the boys. The boy on the Sinner's Sorrow whined piteously and rocked from one knee to the other. The Admiral looked at him and rolled his eyes.

"Oh, back to your block, you baby," he muttered, and the boy jumped up and scrambled back onto his stone block.

The Admiral backed up until he was again in line, shoulder to shoulder with the others in the puddle. He raised his sword and pointed it straight up at the coal-black clouds that rumbled and flashed overhead.

"Work!" he hollered, practically screaming now to be heard over the gusts and crashes and rain. There was a tingling in the air. A buzzing, a charge, a vibration. "Suffering! Discipline! You are dirty little scabs, you devils, and you've been sent to hell!"

As the Admiral spoke, the metal buttons on his jacket began to glow with a strange blue light. There was a crackling, like static all around. Then a great blinding flash.

A hot-white bolt of lightning shot down from the black clouds and through the upheld sword in the Admiral's hand. Spidery lines of electricity surged and cracked through the crowd of adults, and in one blink of a bit of a second, the puddle at their feet burned to a hissing white burst and the world was split by a deafening cannon crack.

The boys screamed and jumped and covered their faces, and Jonathan felt himself thrown off his block and onto his rear on the ground.

Then, all was still. Jonathan sat on the wet stone with his eyes squeezed shut and heard nothing.

Bit by bit, sounds came back. A fading rumble of thunder. The rain dripping on the walls and puddles of the prison. Gusts of wind whistling between the towers. Jonathan lowered his arms and blinked open his eyes.

Two boys still stood on their blocks. The rest were on the ground, like him. They were all looking at where the Admiral and his men had been standing a moment before.

The men were still there. But they all lay in a heap on the ground. Perfectly still. Rain pattered softly on their coats, their boots, their bare hands. The air reeked of steam and burning and electricity and lightning. No one moved.

Slowly—first one, then two, then all of them—the boys crept closer. Step by step they formed a cautious half circle around the pile of grown-ups. No one got too close. There was the Admiral, facedown, his hat on the ground and the sword still in his hand. There was Mr. Warwick, on his back, his one eye open and gaping up at the storm.

"Is he . . ." one of the boys started to say.

"Are they . . ." another began.

There was a crack of thunder and they all jumped, but no one stepped away. They hardly noticed the rain pouring down around them.

"Oh, man. Are they . . . dead?" It was Walter who finally managed to ask the question they were all wondering.

"We need to check," the big kid named Tony said.

"How?" Sebastian asked breathlessly.

Colin took one step closer to the steaming bodies.

"Thomeone needth to check for a pulth."

Sebastian nodded.

"Right. Do it, Colin."

"Me? I don't want—"

"Just do it, Colin. You're closest."

Colin stepped forward. He tiptoed between the bodies like he was afraid they'd wake up. He shied away from Mr. Warwick's staring eye and reached down toward the Admiral. His hand stopped inches from the Admiral's neck and he looked up at Sebastian with wide eyes.

"Do it," Sebastian snapped.

Colin tucked the corners of his mouth into a frown and stretched down the last bit. He felt with his fingers past the Admiral's collar, trying to find the neck. Jonathan cringed and braced himself, expecting the Admiral to leap up at any moment with a furious roar.

But there was no leaping. No fury. No roar.

Colin stood motionless for a moment, his eyes on the ground and his mouth still frowning and the fingers of one hand held to the soggy neck of the Admiral of Slabhenge. Then he blinked and looked up at the boys gathered at a fearful distance around him.

"He'th dead," Colin whispered. "Dead ath a doornail."

CHAPTER SIX
A DARK AND DASTARDLY SCHEME

There was a moment of silence. Jonathan heard someone gulp. Colin realized he was still touching the dead Admiral and yanked his hand back and stood up straight.

"Are they *all* dead?" Tony asked.

"Check 'em, Colin," Sebastian demanded.

"No way, Thebathtian. I did mine. Thomebody elth'th turn." Colin hopped out from between the bodies and rejoined the group.

Sebastian grunted in frustration.

"Fine. Tony, you check those two," he said, pointing at Mr. Warwick and another body. "Benny, those two. And . . . you, Johnny or whatever, you do those ones." He pointed at Jonathan and then at Mr. Mongley and the man who'd bellowed out their names during Muster.

"It's Jonathan, and I—"

"Whatever. Just do it. Now."

Jonathan could tell that arguing wasn't going to work. He wiped his hands on his pant legs and stepped forward.

He checked the roll caller first. The man's eyes were closed, but his mouth was open. Steam was rising off his jacket. Jonathan pressed two fingers against the man's neck. His fingers were half-numb from the cold. He pressed them in harder. It felt like touching a warm steak.

He felt nothing. He waited, quietly. Nothing.

He looked up. "Dead," he said, and stepped over to Mr. Mongley. He heard Tony and Benny reporting the same thing from their dead grown-ups.

Without thinking or pausing, he shoved his fingers into Mr. Mongley's throat. He remembered the man's raspy, haunting breath. Raindrops were running down the old man's bald, flaky scalp. His head was to the side, his eyes both open, staring at the distant gray wall. They were actually kind of a beautiful shade of blue. Jonathan gritted his teeth and tried not to throw up.

The man's neck was still and pulseless.

"Mr. Mongley's dead, too."

He remembered the night before and his whispered conversation with Walter, before the bucket. *Mongley hears everything*, Walter had said. He looked up at Walter.

"Well," Jonathan said hoarsely. "He's not hearing anything now."

Walter's Adam's apple bobbed in a dry swallow.

"Maybe he'th hearing the choirth of angelth thinging," Colin offered.

Walter's eyes were still on the dead man. He shook his head and frowned. "I seriously doubt that, man."

Jonathan straightened up and stepped back into the quiet, watching circle.

"All the grown-ups are dead," Tony said in a hollow, wondering voice.

"Is this *all* of them?" Jonathan asked, his voice rising.

"There's no one else inside? A janitor, or a guard, or something?"

Walter shook his head. "It was Morning Muster. This is all the grown-ups, man. The whole Slabhenge staff."

"Why'd they all die?" Miguel asked.

"The Admiral was holding that sword," Jonathan said.

"And they were all touching," Sebastian added.

"Thtanding in that puddle," Colin finished.

Tony sniffed and looked back at the stone blocks they'd been balancing on when the lightning struck.

"We were on the blocks, up out of the puddles," he said in a trembling voice. "We'd all be dead, too, if we'd-a been standing on the ground."

Jonathan looked at Mr. Warwick's one glassy, dead eye staring sightlessly up at the storm clouds. "Which we weren't, thank the devil," he whispered.

There was a sudden, gusting blast of wind that whipped their hair and clothes around. Thunder cracked and the somber scene of wet children looking at a pile of dead bodies was lit by a long flash of lightning. The rain doubled in strength, rolling up to a real downpour. Suddenly, they each seemed to realize that they themselves were now standing together in a puddle, with the lightning still flashing. One by one, and then all at once, without anyone saying anything, they scurried over to the cover of the big gated doorway that led out to the boat landing. It was cold in the shadows of the stone archway, but it was out of the wind and rain and, most important, the bolts of lightning that darted across the sky.

They huddled together in the near-darkness, looking out at the corpses getting soggy in the courtyard. A couple of the smaller kids were crying. Not because they were sad, Jonathan thought, just scared.

"We're in so much trouble," Benny said.

"What?" Sebastian's voice was harsh and scornful. "What for? We didn't do anything!"

"Still," Miguel said. "Here we are. You know, *us* . . . the 'scabs' and all that. And all the grown-ups end up dead? I mean, my folks sent me here just for skipping school a few times, you know? I'm definitely gonna get grounded for at least a week for this when I get home."

His last word hung in the air between them. The wind couldn't blow it away. *Home.* It dawned on them at the same time.

"We get to go home," Walter said quietly.

"We get to go home," another kid echoed.

"We get to go home!" two or three kids cried. Someone cheered. A few kids clapped. Jonathan bit his bottom lip and frowned. Sebastian cracked his knuckles and furrowed his brow.

"When do we go?" Tony asked. "Can we call now? The police?"

"There's no telephone, idiot," Sebastian said under his breath. He turned his head so that everyone could hear him.

"There's no telephone, remember? No one's going home yet." He looked out at the bodies, his eyes narrowed, and he said it again more quietly. "No one's going home yet."

"Well . . . when can we go?" Tony asked again. "When's the next boat coming?"

They all looked at Benny.

"You worked in his office, Benny. You know the schedule best," a tall, skinny kid with red hair said. Jonathan remembered from Morning Muster that his name was Gerald.

Benny still had his eyes glued to his boss's body. He shook his head.

"Uh, well, today's Tuesday, right? There's no food drop-off or garbage pickup 'til Thursday. No new students are registered to come that I know of. So today would just be Patrick coming on the mail run."

"When's that?"

"Just before lunch, usually. Like ten thirty."

"All right," Walter said. "A couple hours. That's it. Then we tell that mail guy what happened and he sends a bigger boat out and then we're all outta here." A couple boys clapped again.

There were a few seconds of nothing but the sound of rain. One kid leaned against the stone wall. Another coughed.

"So, like . . . what should we do?" Miguel asked.

"Thould we get them out of the rain?" Colin asked.

Jonathan's brain was working. He was looking at all the dead grown-ups and frowning and thinking of home and family and everything that had happened to bring him here to the island of Slabhenge. A small, ugly, beautiful idea was wiggling in his mind. His stomach rumbled, wanting more than a meager bowl of oatmeal. It was hard to hatch a dark and dastardly scheme on an empty stomach.

"I think we should eat," he said, just loud enough for everyone to hear. "I'm starving."

Sebastian's brow was still creased with dark, thoughtful lines.

"Yeah," he said. "I'm with the new kid. Let's go eat." Then his face smoothed into a grinning smile and he cocked an eyebrow back at the huddled boys. "Whatever we want."

One kid clapped. But just one. Most of the boys had probably lost their appetites when they watched all the adults get struck and killed by lightning.

But Sebastian started off across the rain-drenched courtyard toward the kitchen door.

Jonathan stepped out after him.

All the rest slowly followed close behind.

The straggly line of somber, soaked boys snaked right past the lifeless bodies staring up at the storm.

The kitchen was noisy with cooking, but there was not much talking. Mouths were too full for talking most of the time.

Tony stirred a pan of ten scrambled eggs. Jonathan didn't think he planned on sharing. Benny was eating jelly out of the jar with a spoon. Sebastian was shoving a banana in his mouth while frying up six pieces of bacon. The two big brutes—Gregory and Roger, Jonathan remembered—were eating pepperoni slices by the handful, greasy grins on their faces. The little black-haired kid named Jason sat on the floor in the walk-in fridge and gnawed on a brick-size block of cheddar cheese.

Most of the boys just stood around, eating in the kitchen, but some got what they wanted and picked a spot at a table. No one sat at the Admiral's table. Jonathan made himself two gooey peanut butter and jelly sandwiches and joined them, sitting across from Colin and Walter. Another kid sat down next to him, a little taller than him, with glasses and short, curly brown hair.

"Francis, right?" Jonathan asked through a mouthful of peanut butter and jelly.

"Yes. And you're Jonathan. Our newest arrival." Francis held out his hand and Jonathan blinked at him for a second before reaching out and shaking it. Francis had a slight accent, but not a foreign one. He pronounced all of his syllables very precisely. To Jonathan, he sounded like the rich people on TV. "Looks like your stay here has been cut quite short."

"Yeah," Jonathan said, chewing. "Guess so."

"And what terrible wrong did you commit to deserve being sent here?" Francis asked. He was being sarcastic, Jonathan could tell, but he still flinched. He swallowed his bite.

"What did *you* do?" he asked back. Across the table, Colin frowned and took another bite of his apple.

"Oh, hardly anything, really," Francis answered in a bored voice. "I pushed our gardener off the ladder. Honestly, if he hadn't broken his hip, there wouldn't even have been charges."

"Was it an accident?"

Francis shrugged. "No."

"Why did you do it?"

Francis rolled his eyes. "Does it really matter?"

"I guess not."

Francis sighed. "Yes. Well, my father got a top-notch attorney, really quite expensive, but the whole thing happened at our summer house and all the local townspeople were quite up in arms about it. Really screaming for blood. Tried to make it all into some ridiculous wealth-class issue. So . . . here I am. Eating white bread. The damned country judge sent me here."

"That'th a terrible thing to do," Colin said.

"Yes, well, the judge's hands were really quite tied, I'm afraid. It's an elected office. He had to give the people what they wanted."

"I meant it wath a terrible thing to do to the gardener."

"Oh," Francis sniffed. "Well. It didn't end well for me, either, as you see."

They all chewed in silence for a while.

"How does the refrigerator work?" Jonathan asked. Everyone stopped chewing and looked at him. "I mean, there doesn't seem to be electricity here. It's all torches and candles. What's running the fridge and freezer?"

Walter scraped a piece of jelly bean out from between his teeth and looked at it stuck to his finger.

"Oh, there's electricity. There's a coal generator downstairs that we all get to take turns shoveling coal into. Makes just enough juice to run the fridge, freezer, and the Admiral's TV."

"Oh." Jonathan swallowed the last bite of his second sandwich and considered going to make another one. "And the freezer's big, too, like the fridge?"

Walter nodded. "Yeah. A little smaller, I guess, but still a walk-in. Why, man?"

Jonathan shook his head. "No reason. Just wondering."

But Jonathan's head was still buzzing with dark dreams. And he *did* have a reason for asking about the freezer.

Eight reasons, in fact.

The sixteen students of the Slabhenge Reformatory School for Troubled Boys stood at the gate, looking out at the white-capped waves of the ocean. Somewhere out there across the sea was the mainland and home. Home. With meals, parents, beds. A happy place. For most of them.

Sebastian had crept up and unclipped the key ring from Mr. Vander's belt, and they'd opened the heavy wooden door to the outside. They stood in the shadow of the stone arch, looking out at the water and waiting for the boat. The eight bodies still lay in the drizzling rain behind them.

They leaned with their hands holding the rusty iron bars. Some of them still chewed on crusty bread or chunks of cheese.

"How much longer?" a kid asked.

"I told you, any minute," Benny answered.

"What should we say?"

"What do you mean, what should we say? All the grown-ups got killed by lightning and we want to go home. Dummy."

The rain was just a constant gentle tapping now. The thunder and lightning were gone, but the clouds were still night-black and the world was dim and dark.

Then, thin and lost somewhere beneath the sound of the waves smacking the stone walls, there came a low buzzing sound. Like a fly caught between the window and the screen.

"There!" Miguel called out, his voice excited. "There! I see it!" He pointed. Other fingers joined.

"Yeah! I see it!"

"There it is!"

The boat was a dot, still far distant, fighting its way through the wind and the waves. To bring them back to the real world. Jonathan chewed on the inside of his cheek. He looked at Sebastian, leaning in the corner where the gate met the stone wall. Sebastian was the only one besides him who wasn't smiling. His scowl was as grim as the deadly clouds, his eyes as full of dark thoughts as Jonathan's. Their eyes met. Jonathan thought he saw a wet glimmer of tears in Sebastian's eyes before they looked away from his.

All the boys' voices fell silent as they watched the little boat make its way toward their gloomy island.

Jonathan took one deep breath and then spoke his voice into the silence.

"Maybe we shouldn't go."

Heads snapped his way. Sebastian's sour face turned sharply toward him.

"What?" Walter asked.

"Maybe we shouldn't go," Jonathan repeated. "Maybe we shouldn't tell what happened. Yet." Sebastian's eyes stayed locked on his. His jaw clenched. Jonathan cocked a questioning eyebrow at him. And then Sebastian nodded.

"What are you talking about?" a kid asked.

Jonathan raised his voice and put some strength into it.

"I'm talking about staying. Without the grown-ups. Without *any* grown-ups. I'm talking about all of us staying here at Slabhenge. Alone."

CHAPTER SEVEN
DEAD MAN'S COAT

"Stay? Why would we do that?" Francis asked.

"Why shouldn't we?" Jonathan answered. "Were any of us really that happy out there? I mean, we've got a chance here. We can live here. Without grown-ups. Without *rules*. Not forever. Just for a while. We could live here—free. Doing whatever we want."

Eyes blinked at him.

"Think about it," Jonathan argued desperately, knowing the boat was getting closer by the second. "Out there we're just . . . troublemakers. Punks. Here we could be *kings*."

"You're crazy!"

"No, he's not." The voice was Sebastian's. He pushed himself off the wall and faced them all. "He's right. We've got a winning lotto ticket here. And we're just gonna throw it away? Without spending any of it?"

The boys looked back and forth among each other.

"Don't you see?" Sebastian demanded. "How long have we all been here, besides Jonathan? Four weeks? Six weeks? Ten? And all that time, we've been crapped on. Cleaning. Working. Eating garbage. Kneeling on that stupid Sinner's whatever. Sleeping with rats. All 'cause of those jerks. And now . . ." His eyes wandered out to the bodies behind them. "And now they're gone. And we can enjoy this. Eat whatever we want. Whenever we want. Eat the Admiral's chocolate. Watch his TV."

"Use his bathroom," Tony added thoughtfully. "I hear he's got actual toilet paper."

"Sleep in his big, fancy bed," Miguel said.

"Go to bed whenever we want," Walter chipped in.

"With a light on," Jason squeaked.

"Thith ith crathy," Colin interjected. "You're all nuth."

"Don't be such a wussy, Colin," Sebastian said.

"Just for a couple days," Jonathan argued. "Like a little . . . vacation. A vacation from grown-ups. No punishment. No problems."

The tall redhead, Gerald, looked up at the building around them.

"God," he said quietly. "This place *would* be amazing to play hide-and-seek in."

"There's plenty of food," Jonathan said.

They stood quietly, each boy wrestling with his own thoughts.

Colin shook his head and opened his mouth to speak, but Sebastian cut him off.

"We're doing it," he said, his voice hard and decisive. "Just for a little while."

"But . . . the boat's coming," Francis pointed out.

Sebastian scowled and looked out at the ocean.

"We've still got like five minutes," he said. "All he's

coming for is mail. Benny . . . do you know where the mail-bag is?"

"Sure. In the staff room."

"What about the guy, though? Won't he notice . . . something?"

Jonathan shook his head. "When I got dropped off, Mr. Vander didn't even talk to him. He stood in the shadows the whole time."

Sebastian rubbed his chin roughly with his hand.

"But still . . ."

"We have Mr. Vander's jacket and hat," Jonathan said. "Well, we could *get* his jacket and hat." Some kid in the shadows gasped, but Jonathan kept going. "And if Gerald stood on a stool or something, he'd be just as tall. Wearing that hat and jacket, back here in the shadows . . ."

"Let's do it." Sebastian's voice was quick and bossy. "Benny, run and grab the mailbag. Gerald, stay here. Everyone else get around the corner out of sight. New kid, come with me."

There was only a momentary pause and then everyone scrambled. Colin was the only one who stayed where he was.

"Thith ith tho thtupid," he said to no one in particular. Sebastian grabbed him roughly by his shirt and jerked him around the corner so hard his head snapped back on his neck. He slammed him up against the stone wall. He pressed his forearm hard into Colin's chest and leaned in close to his face.

"Don't mess this up for the rest of us, you little jerk," Sebastian growled. "You do, you're dead."

"Hey," Jonathan said. "Take it easy, man. He's cool."

Sebastian snorted. "There's *nothing* cool about this little dweeb," he said.

"Come on," Jonathan said. "Let him go. We gotta hurry."

Sebastian gave Colin one last glare, then followed Jonathan out toward the heap of bodies. They stood together for a second, looking at the corpse of Mr. Vander lying in the middle of the pile.

"You really think we can do this, Johnny?"

"Jonathan. And it's worth a try."

There was no time to be queasy or delicate. Sebastian knelt down next to the tall, still form and started pulling at his long, blue coat.

"Damn! It's buttoned! Help me, will you?"

Together they frantically yanked the buttons through their holes. Jonathan kept his eyes on his fingers and away from the dead man's face. They did wander once, though— he saw the mouth half-open, a bit of dry gray tongue poking out, saw a raindrop roll off the forehead, saw the swirling storm above reflected in the cloudy, unfocused eyes—and he almost lost it. His breath caught, his fingers fumbled . . . but he blinked and looked away and kept going.

With the buttons undone, the boys started pulling the arms out of the sleeves. Mr. Vander's arms were incredibly heavy and stiff. Sebastian and Jonathan tugged and wiggled and jerked. Mr. Vander's head lolled and rocked from side to side, loose and floppy. Jonathan clenched his stomach and kept his eyes on his work.

"God," Sebastian panted. "And I thought I hated this guy when he was *alive*!"

They got one arm loose and, with a grunting heave, they rolled Mr. Vander over onto his stomach to work on the other. His face smacked against the stone ground with a sickening thud. Sebastian grabbed the cuff of the second sleeve and gave it a swift yank like a magician whipping the tablecloth off a table full of dishes. The jacket pulled free and Sebastian fell back onto his butt in a puddle.

"Grab his hat, Johnny."

They raced back toward the gate, Jonathan holding the hat, and the coat stuffed under Sebastian's arm.

Gerald stood alone, scratching at his neck and looking uncomfortable.

"Put this on!" Sebastian hollered, tossing Mr. Vander's jacket to him. He ducked low and peered out the gate. "He's almost here!"

"Man, I don't know if I want to put on a dead guy's coat."

Sebastian shot him a dark look.

"Don't put it on and you'll *be* a dead guy. Do it. All you gotta do is stand here in the shadows. Big deal."

Benny ran up huffing and puffing, a canvas bag slung over his shoulder. He tossed it on the ground at Sebastian's feet.

Gerald grimaced and pulled the long coat on. He

pinched it between his fingers like a dirty diaper. The bottom of the coat piled on the ground. Jonathan gave him an apologetic look and handed him the hat. Gerald closed his eyes and plopped it on his head. It dropped down onto his ears.

Sebastian stepped back to take a look at him. Behind them the sound of the boat got louder.

"Shoot!" Sebastian exclaimed. "We forgot the stool! You're way too short!" He looked frantically around for something for Gerald to stand on.

Jonathan thought fast. He dropped to his hands and knees in the shadows just inside the gate.

"He can stand on me," he said. "But make sure the coat covers me up."

Sebastian pulled Gerald over and he stepped gingerly up onto Jonathan's back. He was a lot heavier than Jonathan had expected. The hard stone blocks ground into his kneecaps. He felt Sebastian adjusting the long trench coat as best he could to cover him.

"Wait!" Gerald protested. "How am I gonna get the mailbag? And give him ours?"

Outside, the motor got louder, then quieter as the gas was cut back.

"Sebastian!" Jonathan hissed from the ground. "You do the bags. And try to stand between him and us!"

"All right."

"What do I do if he talks to me?" Gerald asked, his voice high and fast.

"Just grunt," Jonathan answered.

"He's here," Sebastian said. "Showtime." Jonathan lowered his head and peeked out from beneath the coat.

The dingy metal boat was just pulling up to the algae-covered stone steps. It was the same boat that had dropped Jonathan off the day before, but this time, Patrick was alone.

"Hello, Mr. Vander!" Patrick shouted good-naturedly as the boat bumped up to the stairs. Gerald didn't reply. Patrick leapt expertly out of the boat onto the steps, a rope tied to the boat in one hand and a canvas bag over his shoulder. Sebastian stepped down to meet him, the mailbag in his hand.

"I'll trade ye," Patrick said with a smile. Sebastian just held the bag out. Patrick shrugged and took it, then handed his own to Sebastian. "What'd ye do to get the supreme honor of being Mr. Vander's little helper?" he asked with a wink.

Sebastian froze. "I . . . I . . . nothing."

Jonathan winced from underneath Gerald.

Patrick squinted at Sebastian. "Ah. Well. Bet ye won't be doin' that again, now, will ye?" He looked past Sebastian, up to where Gerald stood atop Jonathan.

"How are ye there today, Mr. Vander?"

Gerald grunted. It sounded a little high and nervous to Jonathan. But Patrick only nodded and smiled with half his mouth. "Good to hear it."

They all stood for a moment looking at each other.

Patrick cocked an eyebrow.

"Well," he said. "Guess I best be off. Can't stand here jabbering with ye all day, Mr. Vander." He raised one hand to his forehead in a little salute and then waved. "Give me best to the Admiral, won't ye?"

Gerald grunted again.

Patrick laughed and hopped into the boat. Looking back over his shoulder, he threw the boat into reverse and receded slowly away against the incoming waves.

All three boys watched him, holding their breath. When he was far enough out, Patrick whipped the boat around and gunned it, chugging toward the mainland. He didn't look back.

Sebastian turned and walked up the stairs, a triumphant sneer on his face. "Nothing to it," he said. Jonathan rolled his eyes.

Gerald hopped down from Jonathan's back and tore the coat off like it was crawling with spiders. He threw the hat down on top of it.

"I'm *never* doing that again!" he cried.

Sebastian snorted and swung the big wooden door closed. "Yeah, you are. Mail comes tomorrow, too, you know." Gerald's shoulders slumped.

All the other boys were gathering around them. The rain had mostly stopped.

Sebastian stood shoulder to shoulder with Jonathan. He still had the cocky smile on his face.

"Well, boys, here we are," he said. "Got the place all to ourselves. You're welcome."

They all stood looking at one another. A seagull shrieked from the top of the wall above them.

"Well, then," Francis said, clearing his throat. "What should we do now?"

Sebastiàn looked at Jonathan and smiled, then looked back at the circle of questioning faces.

"Whatever the hell we want," he said, and his grin widened even more. He cracked his knuckles and started walking through the circle, toward the door to the main building across the courtyard.

"Uh, Thebathtian?" Colin called after him, stopping him in mid-step. "What about the bodieth?"

CHAPTER EIGHT
DRAGGING THE DEAD

They all turned and looked at the pile of soggy corpses. Sebastian stood with his mouth open, his eyebrows frowning.

Jonathan had already thought that through.

"The freezer," he said. "Otherwise, they'll—" He stopped and grimaced, then shrugged. "We have to put them in the freezer."

Sebastian nodded at him. "That makes sense," he said.

"The freezer's a long ways away," Tony said.

Sebastian raised his eyebrows at him. "Then we better get started."

Sebastian did the math of eight bodies and sixteen boys and assigned each body to two boys. None of the pairs could get their body more than a few feet before dropping it with a stomach-twisting, meaty splash in a puddle, though.

Dead bodies are heavy, it turns out. When they're wearing rain-drenched coats and wool trousers, they're really heavy. And when they're rain-soaked bodies of men being carried by a bunch of kids who don't even really want to touch them, they're almost impossibly heavy.

"Okay," Sebastian barked, gasping for breath and still holding Mr. Warwick's feet in his hands. "Two trips. Four people per body. Someone take one of these legs."

The bodies were still heavy, but in teams of four, they at least managed to drag them toward the door. It was tough going, though. Curses and accusations echoed around the courtyard.

"Come on! You're only *pretending* to hold that arm!"

"Lift higher! It's hard to pull when his head's dragging like that!"

"I *am* trying, Jason! His ankle is just too slippery!"

"No, not by the elbow, dummy! Grab under the armpits! Like this!"

"Gross! His tongue touched me!"

But, step by step, they got the bodies out of the courtyard and through the door and down the dark hallway and into the room where they'd eaten breakfast. The groups were spread out by then, depending on how big a body they'd gotten stuck with. Jonathan was with Colin, Miguel, and the kid named David. They, unfortunately, had ended up with the Admiral, and they were at the very end of the morbid, sweating, swearing parade.

"Dang, man," Miguel panted, wrestling with a leg that was slippery with rain. "Why'd I get stuck with three of the littlest guys?"

David, who was trying to get a good grip on the Admiral's right arm, shot him a look.

"I ain't no weakling."

"Nah, nah, you know what I mean," Miguel said quickly. "We all know you tough. That's why you're here, right? For being all tough and stuff and, like, almost killing some guy or something?"

Jonathan glanced nervously at David, but David just rolled his eyes.

"No. Just for fighting."

"Yeah," Miguel said. "But, like, a *lot* of fighting, right?"

David shrugged. They struggled for a few more steps in silence, but then he spoke again, his quiet voice a rush of frustration.

"I'm the only Japanese kid at my school, right? And every day—*every day*—they make fun of me. They push. They throw things. Whisper things. And so, yes, I fight back. So I get lots of practice, right? So, after a while, I start to win. And what's wrong with that? So some . . . some . . . *moron* starts up again and ends up with a broken jaw and a concussion and I'm supposed to be sorry? The judge says"—David bitterly slipped into a deep, adult voice—" 'All these terrible fights, all these stitches and broken noses, and *you* are the common denominator.' Me? I laughed at the judge. 'Cause from where I was sitting, the common denominator was all those stupid white boys."

Miguel dropped the Admiral's leg and straightened up to catch his breath.

"Sure, man," he said. "Whatever you say. You're on top. You're the *numerator,* man. Just remember I ain't white next time you start swinging, okay, champ?"

David scowled.

"What about you?" he asked. "What are you in for?"

Miguel shrugged.

"Eh. Truancy. I'm not, like, super great at showing up to school, you know? My folks *chose* to send me here, to fix my attitude. Can you believe that?" A grin spread across his face. "But look at me now! *Choosing* to stay here, when we could go home! I'm reformed!"

He looked around at them, waiting for a laugh, but they were all too tired and out of breath. Jonathan gave him a little smile and wiped the sweat from his forehead.

"What about you, newbie?" Miguel asked. "What'd you do to get yourself sent here?"

Jonathan's smile flickered away. His eyes dropped away from Miguel's. The Admiral was looking up at him, his foul mouth open and his dead eyes gaping.

"Come on," Jonathan said. "Let's get this over with. This guy ain't getting any lighter."

The boys stooped and regained their holds and hoisted the Admiral up with a chorus of grunts and curses.

"Thith ith abtholutely inthane," Colin complained under his breath, changing his grip around the Admiral's left armpit. "We thould've told right away."

"I'd keep that to yourself," Jonathan murmured, looking up the hallway. "I think Sebastian'll actually kick your butt if you keep talking like that." Jonathan was holding the Admiral's other limp arm and dragging him backward. Walter and David each had a leg.

"Thebathian? Thith wath all *your* idea, Jonathan."

Jonathan frowned and cleared his throat. The Admiral's head rocked from side to side as they walked, looking back and forth from him to Colin like he was listening to the conversation. Jonathan tried to avoid the Admiral's glassy, staring eyes.

"Yeah, well, I was right. I didn't want to go home." The Admiral's head flopped over to Colin.

"Well, thome of uth *do*." The Admiral's head flopped back to Jonathan.

Jonathan didn't know what to say. He looked away from the Admiral's accusing eyes.

"It's just for a few days, Colin," he said through gritted teeth. His fingers were burning from the Admiral's weight. "Just relax. It'll be fun." The Admiral's corpse looked back to Colin. His tongue was starting to stick out.

"Fun? With *him* in charge? He'll be worth than the Admiral!" Colin looked down at the Admiral's empty stare. "No offenth."

"Sebastian's not in charge," Jonathan assured him. "No one is. It's just all of us. He's not taking over."

Colin looked up into Jonathan's eyes and frowned his little frown.

"Jutht wait and thee." He shook his head. "The inmateth are running the athylum."

"The inmates are running the asylum? What does that mean?"

Colin shrugged. "It'th jutht a thaying."

"Who says it?"

"People."

"When do they say it?" The Admiral's head rocked back over to look at Jonathan.

Colin sighed and put his shoulder under the Admiral's uncooperative arm.

"When everything thtarth to go wrong."

By then, some of the boys had already made it to the freezer and dropped their bodies off. They walked out of the kitchen, red-faced and sweaty. Sebastian was among them.

"Listen up," he called out, panting. "Once you get both your bodies put away, we're gonna meet at the big table. We need to decide some stuff. And hurry up."

Colin shot Jonathan a meaningful look that he pretended not to see.

Finally, they got the Admiral's bloated body to the freezer. Their breath puffed in frosty clouds as they dragged and pushed him up onto the pile of corpses.

Jonathan was the last to leave. He slipped gratefully out of the freezer but groaned when the door hit the Admiral's jutting boot, six inches shy of closing. Colin and the others were already out the freezer door and into the kitchen, heading back for the next corpse.

He kicked at the Admiral's boot but his leg was stiff and the boot wouldn't budge. He sighed and looked over his shoulder and reluctantly walked back into the freezer. He grabbed the Admiral under both armpits and heaved, trying to twist him over and higher up on the pile of bodies. As he did so, he heard a metallic clanging and looked down.

A key had fallen out of the Admiral's jacket pocket. It was a big key, rusty and old-fashioned. Jonathan glanced around and shivered. He picked up the key and slipped it into his pocket, then gave the Admiral one last push to clear the door and walked out to rejoin the rest of the boys.

CHAPTER NINE
SCAR ISLAND

"Okay," Sebastian began when they all met at the table, exhausted and limp from dragging dead bodies across a hundred yards of stone. "First things first. I'm in charge."

Colin turned his head to give Jonathan a *very* meaningful look. Jonathan bit his tongue and didn't look back.

Sebastian was sitting in the Admiral's big wooden chair, his feet up on the table. Benny was sitting next to him, with Roger and Gregory nearby.

"Why are you in charge?" Tony asked.

"Because I say so, Tony. We can't have *no one* in charge. It'd be dumb. And I've been here the longest. And I'm the oldest."

"I'm older than you are," Gerald protested.

"Shut up, Gerald. I'm in charge. Anyone have a problem with that?"

"Do we have another choith?"

"No."

"Could we have electionth?"

"No. And you better shut up right now, Colin."

"*Let it go,*" Jonathan whispered through clenched teeth, nudging Colin. "*It'll be fine.*"

Colin just shook his head and frowned. His hand flitted up to pinch nervously at his neck.

"Okay, now that's settled. First rule is . . ." Sebastian

smiled like a cat with a mouthful of feathers. He spread his hands wide. ". . . there are no rules."

There was a little scattered clapping among the group. Some nervous laughter. Sebastian looked around at them, a little frown on his face.

"Why do you guys look so scared?"

No one answered. Eyes dropped to the floor.

"What's wrong with you guys? This is the best thing that ever happened to us!"

There was still no answer except the sound of the rain still pattering in the courtyard outside the window.

Sebastian jumped to his feet.

"What? You think we can't do this? You think we can't take care of ourselves and have fun?" Sebastian shook his head.

"Come on! The stupid Admiral? He called us scabs, right?" Sebastian's face darkened. "Picked off and thrown away, he said. But now he's gone. And here *we* are. Still around. 'Cause you know what you get when you keep picking at a scab?"

He looked around at them, his eyes shining.

"Bloody fingers?" Miguel suggested.

"An infection?" Walter asked.

"No!" Sebastian spat. "You get a *scar*, idiots. A scar. And scars are tough. The Admiral was wrong. We ain't scabs. We're *scars*."

"Yeah!" Benny piped up eagerly. "Scars, man!"

Jonathan's stomach suddenly twisted and tightened. He blinked quickly and rubbed at his sleeves with sweaty palms.

Sebastian's mouth spread into a grin and he opened his arms wide.

"Look around, guys! This whole place belongs to us. We're the kings. No one to boss us around. No one to get us in trouble. It's *our* island now. Ours. We don't need nobody. 'Cause we're Scars now. Scars with a capital *S*. The tough Scars that got left behind. It's *our* island."

"Hell yeah!" Roger cheered in his deep voice. "*Our* island!"

"Our island!" Gregory echoed.

Sebastian slammed his fist down on the table, his face glowing with triumph.

"This whole island belongs to the Scars now!"

"Scar Island!" Benny crowed.

Sebastian had them now. There were cheers and smiles and high fives. Even Walter was nodding his head and grinning.

"This ain't Slabhenge anymore!" Sebastian hollered. "It's Scar Island from now on! Say it!"

"Scar Island!" all the boys shouted.

All the boys except Colin, who just sat looking around, pale and frowning.

And all the boys except Jonathan, still rubbing his arms and blinking.

Sebastian sat back down, his face flushed.

"The jerks are gone," he said. "We can do. Whatever. We. Want."

There was more clapping, more cheering.

"Except . . . we should eat meals together, I think," Sebastian added. "To check in. Make sure we're all okay. That makes sense, right?" He looked at Jonathan. Jonathan dropped his hands quickly from his arms. He shrugged and nodded.

"So do whatever you want, guys. Run around. Eat some more. Whatever. But be back here for dinner. Have fun, Scars."

Everyone sat and looked at each other for a moment. Then Francis stood up and started toward the kitchen. David got up and headed for the door that led outside.

"Wait," Jonathan said. "What about the generator? We still need electricity, right? For the fridge and the . . . freezer?"

Sebastian pursed his lips. "Oh, yeah. Right. We'll, uh, take turns. It only has to get done, what, like three times a day?" He looked to Benny, who nodded eagerly. "We've all done it, we know how it works. So, first, how about . . . you and you," he said, pointing at Miguel and another kid Jonathan didn't know yet. "Head down and fill it up." They grumbled and trudged away together.

Slowly the rest of the boys wandered away in different directions, most in groups of two or three. Sebastian headed out into the courtyard. Benny followed like a puppy at his heels.

Colin and Walter and Jonathan were the last left at the tables. Colin still looked unhappy.

"Cheer up," Jonathan said to him. "Now the good times start." Colin just rolled his eyes.

"So . . . what is there to do around here?" Jonathan asked.

It was Walter's turn to roll his eyes. "Who knows? All we

ever did was work, man. Mop the floors, clean the kitchen, scrub the toilets. I've been here weeks and I bet I ain't seen any more of the place than you have."

"Well, then," Jonathan said, standing up. "Let's go exploring."

Walter hopped up to join him, and after a moment Colin did, too.

"We're gonna need lanternth," Colin said with a sigh. "I know where they keep them. Matcheth, too."

A few minutes later, the three of them were walking through one of the snaking, shadowy hallways that had been so confusing to Jonathan the night before. Jonathan and Walter each held a hissing lantern.

"This place is like a maze," Jonathan said, moving his lantern from side to side to banish suspicious shadows in the corners.

"It *is* a maze," Walter said. "I heard they built it that way on purpose, to confuse the crazies. So only the guards would know their way around, you know?"

Jonathan slipped on an especially slimy stair and, putting out his hand to catch himself, almost grabbed a huge brown rat. He jerked his hand back and the rat squeaked angrily and slithered into a hole between two blocks.

"Well," he said, standing up. "If they weren't crazy when they got here, I bet it didn't take too long to get that way."

Walter looked uneasily at the hole the rat had disappeared into.

"Yeah, man. You got that right." He shook his shoulders in an exaggerated shiver. "This place gives me the heebie-jeebies. Thinking about all them crazies that lived here. And died here." He dropped his voice to a whisper. It echoed in the corridor like turning pages. He looked from Jonathan to Colin. "You guys believe in ghosts?"

Colin shook his head, but he didn't look so sure.

"I don't know," Jonathan said, squinting into the blackness ahead of them. "But if there are ghosts, this sure seems like the kind of place they'd be."

"Yeah," Walter answered. "No lie." He looked at Jonathan. He had second thoughts written all over his face.

Jonathan put on a smile that was a lot braver than he felt. "Well, let's go find 'em, then."

Walter shook his head and almost smiled.

"Fine. I'm following you, though."

They wandered up and down staircases and peeked into sinister-looking side passages. Jonathan was hopelessly lost within minutes. They found one room they were pretty sure used to be some sort of dungeon; rusted chains dangled from the walls. They took a quick look and then kept going.

Suddenly, the light of Jonathan's lantern fell on something familiar. It was a rope, stretched across a staircase spiraling down into darkness.

"Hey! I know where we are! Mr. Warwick showed this to me."

Colin and Walter stood shoulder to shoulder with him.

"Yeah," Colin whispered. "He loved to try and thcare uth with thith."

"The door to the deep, he called it," Walter said in a low voice.

"The Hatch." Jonathan nodded. "What's really down there?" He felt both Walter and Colin shrug beside him.

"No one knows, man," Walter whispered. "They'd never tell us. Some big, dark secret, I guess." From the stairs rose the same thumping and slurping Jonathan had heard the night before. He swallowed, then stepped forward and lifted the rope. He ducked his head beneath it and stepped down onto the top stair.

"What are you doing?" Colin hissed.

"I wanna see it," Jonathan answered.

He took another step down, then another, holding his lantern out before him. When he didn't hear any footsteps behind him, he looked back. Colin and Walter were still standing on the other side of the rope in the corridor.

"Come on," he whispered. His voice echoed eerily in the tight staircase. "Don't make me go alone. Things are always bigger and darker when they're secret. Let's find out how bad it really is."

Walter gulped. Then he ducked under the rope and followed Jonathan.

"No way," Colin said. "I'm thtaying here."

"Suit yourself," Jonathan said. "But we've got both lanterns."

Colin scooted under the rope and joined Walter. "Jerkth."

Jonathan reached back to pat Colin on the shoulder.

"Relax," he said. "Whatever's down here can't be worse than the dead Admiral, and we spent plenty of time with *him* today."

"Thut up and go."

The stairs were steep, and the boys held one hand against the slippery wall to steady themselves. The steps curved down around a corner and then stopped at a small, dark landing. The landing was a little bigger than a bed, and on the other side, another staircase climbed up and away from them, in the opposite direction of the one they'd come down. On one wall of the landing was another doorway, smaller and rounded on top.

The scraping, slurping, knocking sounds were coming from the smaller doorway. They were louder here, closer. Goose bumps popped out on Jonathan's arms. He held his lantern as far out in front of himself as he could toward the doorway.

Through the doorway was another staircase. It dropped down into even deeper darkness. The lantern's light couldn't reach the end of it.

He felt Colin breathing in one of his ears, and Walter in the other, looking over his shoulder.

"I ain't going any farther," Walter whispered. The darkness down the doorway sloshed and chunked.

"Me neither," Colin breathed.

"Fine," Jonathan said. "I'll go by myself."

"Why?" Colin asked. "Why don't we jutht go back, Jonathan?"

Jonathan stared down into the blackness. He answered without turning his head. His voice echoed back at him from the dark downward passageway, like he was talking to himself.

"It's this big, awful secret, right? The Hatch, down here in the dark? Well, maybe, once you know it, it's not all that terrible after all."

He looked back over his shoulder and locked eyes with Walter.

"Maybe it's the hiding that makes it horrible, you know?"

Walter furrowed his brow.

"Uhh . . . not really, man. I think we should get outta here. Like, *fast.*"

Jonathan turned back toward the rattling, grinding blackness. "Big, dark secrets can't stay that way forever," he murmured. His free hand rubbed absently at the wrist that was holding the lantern.

A dull, heavy thud echoed up the stairway toward them.

"Jonathan?" Walter's whisper was right in his ear. "I am really, really, really"—he paused—"hungry. When you're done playing with the monsters, you can find me in the kitchen, eating sausage."

"I'll be with him," Colin added.

"Thanks, guys," Jonathan said, and his only answer was the sound of their footsteps retreating back up the spiral staircase.

He held the lantern in a shaking hand and shuffled to the end of the landing, to the very edge of the final staircase. This one was narrower than the other corridors; the walls weren't much farther apart than Jonathan's shoulders.

Jonathan took a deep breath. Before him, there was another loud clunk, and a snuffling sound like a huge hissing nose. When he blew his breath out, it came out shaky.

He took the first step down. The steps were bigger drops down than the other staircase. He had to fall the last couple of inches. He took the next step down. He almost turned and ran when an especially loud metal rattling rang up from the darkness below. But he licked his lips and took a breath and dropped down another step. And another.

The darkness before him growled and crunched. The walls seemed to close in around him. He felt with his foot for the next step and realized that he was at the bottom. And that somewhere along the line, he had squeezed his eyes shut.

He opened his eyes.

He was in a tiny square room with a stone ceiling so low he could've reached up and touched it. It was freezing, and the walls were covered in dripping moisture as if they were sweating.

In front of him was a huge, round, metal door. Heavy iron bolts circled its outer edge. It was rusty and grimy and covered in shiny, green slime. It looked ancient. The door was big enough that, if it had been open (and he was extremely thankful that it wasn't), he could have stepped through it without ducking. It was a door like a submarine would have, with the large iron handle in the middle that Jonathan knew would open the door if he spun it around.

The door seemed to rattle rhythmically, like it was breathing.

"The Hatch," Jonathan whispered. He stepped toward it. He reached out with his empty hand. He could see the trembling in his fingers. They closed around the iron handle in the center of the door.

As his fingers touched the metal, his eyes dropped down to a round shadow at the foot of the door. The wavering light from his lantern flashed across it.

A human skull, white bone spotted with green slime, propped against the grimy stone doorway, black eye sockets gaping right at him, toothy mouth frozen in a silent scream.

The door suddenly rocked and banged against his shaking hand. There was a tremendous crack and a wet, sloshing thud, and a freezing mist sprayed Jonathan in the face.

He screamed and fell back, slipping on the wet stone. The lantern dropped from his hand and landed on the hard floor with a shattering crash.

The light went out, plunging Jonathan into absolute, eye-choking darkness.

CHAPTER TEN
A VOICE IN THE DARK

Jonathan crouched on his hands and knees, panting in the blackness. He'd never seen such darkness before, so total and suffocating. Down in the deepest dungeon, pinned beneath a prison of dark stone, there was hardly even the memory of light. His eyes gasped like the mouth of a fish yanked out of the water. They found no light to breathe.

He waited for arms to wrap around his waist, long scaly fingers to close around his throat, teeth to pierce his shaking flesh. But one panicked breath passed. Then another.

All there was was complete darkness and the sound of his fear-gasping lungs and the same rhythmic watery thuds and sloshes of the Hatch. The stone under his hands was moist and clammy. The frigid, hard floor began to hurt his knees. His racing heart began to slow down, just enough for him to start to think. He tried to slow his lungs down.

He felt with his hands and found the lantern. The glass was broken and he shook and tapped it, but he knew that restarting it in the dark was impossible.

He was lost. In the dungeon of an asylum. In total darkness. With a skull. He couldn't help but wonder where the rest of the body was.

"*Crap*," he whispered, and tried not to freak out. Still on his hands and knees, he turned around and started crawling up the stairs, away from the Hatch, his hands feeling through the inky black mystery in front of him.

He found the steep stairs and tumbled up them, bumping his knees and knocking his elbow on the stone wall. Behind him, the Hatch rumbled and chomped. He scrambled faster, climbing up the staircase to the landing. He tripped on the last step and fell, twisting onto his back. Something scrabbled away from him in the darkness on sharp claws. It sounded big.

Gasping, he jumped to his feet and felt around for the walls. His breaths came fast and shallow. His heartbeat drummed in his head. He staggered with his hands reaching out in front of him like a blind man, until his foot hit a stair and he fell again onto brutal stone. With the Hatch behind him thumping as loudly as his heart in his ears, he raced up them in a stumbling crawl. He got to the top and felt a corner, a turn, and he shuffled with feeling fingers around it. The noise of the Hatch got quieter. He kept one hand on the wall to his right and fumbled down a long corridor until he could no longer hear the Hatch at all. He was still in absolute blackness, his eyes blinking and rolling and seeing nothing.

He stopped for a moment to catch his breath and calm down, leaning against the wet stone wall. He dropped his head against the wall and sucked in great gasps of the musty air and blew it out through round lips until his lungs weren't heaving and his heart was merely pumping and not pounding.

Then he remembered: *the rope!* He'd never ducked under or run into the rope stretched across the top of the stairwell. Which could mean only one thing: He'd gone the wrong way. After his spinning fall on the landing, he must have stumbled up the wrong staircase, the one that had led in the opposite direction of the one he and Walter and Colin had come down.

He gulped and his breath started speeding up again. He'd have to backtrack, back down past the seething Hatch.

Or go forward. Into darkness and mystery and unexplored passages.

Behind him, dimly, he heard a sharp bang and grumble. The Hatch. It was just a door. A rusty, wet door of ancient iron that held something back. But for some reason, Jonathan felt like it was waiting for him. Hungry, in the dark.

He clenched his teeth and took a step forward.

The corridor was straight for a while, ten or fifteen steps. His fingers found one doorway, closed with a wooden door so rotten it crumbled under his fingertips, but he continued past it. At the end of the straightaway, the hall turned in a sharp L to the right, and Jonathan scooted around the corner. He stopped and listened, hoping to hear the voices of the other boys or even the sound of the ocean, which would mean a window or a door to the outside. But there was only the always-and-everywhere sound of water dripping, and his own echoey breaths, and the occasional distant scratching of claws in the dark.

He took a step forward and the world was gone. His foot found only air beneath it and he tried to catch himself on the wall, but there was no grip on the slimy surface and he fell forward with a scream.

Dank air whistled past his face. He thrust his arms desperately out in front of him and then he slammed with horrible force onto a down staircase, the edges of the stairs like sharpened fists hammering his body. He slid and rolled and bounced down the stairs, each stair yanking a grunt or a groan from him.

At the bottom, gasping in blackness, he lay with his cheek in a cold puddle and felt each pain and pulse in his body. He flexed his fingers. Wiggled his toes. Bent his knees and elbows.

"Nothing's broken," he said out loud. His voice sounded small and alone in all that empty darkness. There was the rusty taste of blood in his mouth.

He was just pushing himself up to his hands and knees when he saw it. He froze in mid-crouch and tried to blink it away—but it was still there.

Light.

A thin line of light, glowing somewhere off ahead of him. With nothing else in the blackness for his eyes to compare it to, he couldn't tell if it was just out of reach of his fingers or fifty feet away. But it was there, shining in the darkness.

He started crawling toward it, his knees and palms

splashing through grimy puddles. The light got clearer, more solid around the edges.

The line of light was coming from under a door.

As he watched, a shadow moved across it, then was gone. Someone or something was moving on the other side of the door. Jonathan strained his ears for a sound, a voice, a laugh. Was it the other boys, the Scars . . . Had he circled around in the darkness back to where he had started?

He couldn't hear anything. Except, maybe, a low humming. He rose to his feet and took a step closer, then two more. Water leaked into his shoes.

There it was again, a deep humming song. He didn't know the tune. But it definitely wasn't one of the Scars.

It was the voice of a grown-up.

He took one final step up to the door.

His foot came down on a teetering pile of something stacked just outside the door. They clattered and crashed to the floor, shattering and skittering on the stones.

The humming stopped. There was a grunt and a growl from behind the door.

Jonathan took one step back but then froze.

The door jerked inward, flooding the corridor with yellow light.

Jonathan's eyes burned and he threw his arm over his face.

A deep, rumbling voice like wet boulders scraping together rasped out of the blinding light.

"What are *you* doing here?"

CHAPTER ELEVEN
A BEAUTIFUL RAT

Jonathan stood pinned in the light. He blinked his eyes and squinted up at the looming shadow before him.

"I'm—I'm just—" He took another step back, but a hand reached out and grabbed hold of his sleeve.

"Get in here," the voice rumbled. "Otherwise *they* will."

Jonathan was pulled by his arm through the door. It slammed shut behind him and the hand released him. He shrank back against the closed door.

The light in the room wasn't as bright as it had first seemed, after his stumbling nightmare in the total darkness. It was just candles, eight or nine of them, and one sputtering lantern.

Jonathan blinked and looked around. The room was full of—*books*. Shelves lined the stone walls, each covered end to end with large, leather-bound books. Low bookshelves divided the middle of the room, also full of neatly lined volumes, with more books standing up on top between heavy iron bookends. Along one long wall were evenly spaced window wells, deep and arched, but their views were blocked by leaning rows of books standing on their sills.

Jonathan knew in an instant that he'd stumbled into Slabhenge's library. And it had a librarian.

He eyed the flickering candles nervously. A bunch of candles in a room full of books didn't seem like a great idea, even in a prison made entirely of stone. He resisted the urge to jump and blow them out.

"Come for a book, did ye? Come to see? What we have?"

Jonathan looked to the source of the voice. The man was old. Incredibly old. Impossibly old. His face was deeply lined with wrinkles and creases. He was thin, and must have once been very tall, before he'd gotten so stooped over. He peered at Jonathan from behind thick, smudged glasses that magnified his eyes to silver dollars, shiny blue. His hair was thin and pure white and long, draping over his shoulders and far down his back.

He held his head to the side and tilted down, so his eyes had to look up into Jonathan's. A shy smile snuck onto his lips, revealing small, crooked, yellow teeth, but the smile scurried quickly away into the shadows.

"Or else *who* will get in?" Jonathan finally managed to croak.

The man's eyebrows crinkled and he frowned.

"I'm sorry?"

"When you—pulled me in. You said to get in or else they would. Who?"

The man's smile returned and stayed. He leaned a little closer to Jonathan.

"Why, the rats. Of course. *They* will. Come in. And we don't like them to."

Jonathan licked his lips and looked away from the man's eerie smile and shining eyes.

"No. I guess not."

"It's been a long time," the man said. "A very long time. Since we've had a visitor. That wasn't a rat."

Jonathan just stood there, blinking stupidly. His mind was still wandering in the dark in a world where all the grown-ups were dead.

"Go ahead. Take a look. Around. Pick one out. Or two." The man's little smile came and went as he spoke, like a bobbing lantern on a boat lost in the fog. He took a step back and spread his arms. "Any book you like."

Jonathan took a breath, then stepped past him and into the shelves of Slabhenge's library.

The books were all old. Their spines were cracked and painted with the gold words of their titles. Some of them Jonathan recognized. Most he did not. Their pages were yellowed and worn. The smell of leather and ink and old paper mixed and mingled with the candlelight and filled the room. All the books, despite their age, shone with a well-cared-for light—there were no cobwebs in this forgotten library, no dust on these ancient books.

"What do ye like? To read?" The librarian's voice trailed along behind him as he scanned the shelves. "Adventure, is it? Jonathan Swift? Mysteries, perhaps? Sherlock Holmes?"

"I used to read a lot," Jonathan answered softly, his eyes exploring the titles of the books as his finger slid over their spines.

"Before? Coming here?"

"Not exactly. Just . . . before."

Jonathan's finger stopped on a dark, well-worn spine. The librarian leaned in to see where Jonathan was looking. He stayed there, his face close to Jonathan's.

"Ah. *Hamlet*. A play, that is. By Shakespeare, of course. A good one. Dark. A prince. A ghost. A murder in a castle. And poor Ophelia. Hamlet loved her. But he thought it was his fault. Her dying." The librarian sighed. "To be. Or not. To be."

Jonathan pursed his lips and kept walking. He suddenly didn't feel like any book at all. He felt like being back where all the grown-ups were dead.

"I've gotta go. Thanks."

"But ye've got no book!"

"It's all right. I don't need one."

The librarian gave him a long, steady look. "We want you to. Take a book. Don't worry about the Admiral. And his rules. These books are for reading."

Jonathan's mind raced. The old librarian didn't know about the Admiral. About the lightning.

"Are you always here, just — by yourself?"

The librarian smiled his fleeting smile again. "Oh, yes. Yes. We are always alone. We don't like them. The Admiral. The others. And they don't like us."

"When's the—last time you saw them?"

The old man shrugged and looked away, scanning the shelves. "Don't know. Three. Four, maybe."

"Four days? Without seeing anyone?"

The librarian smiled a wide, staying smile. He looked up at Jonathan in his strange, sideways way.

"No, no. Four *years*. Four years without seeing. Anyone. At least."

Jonathan's mouth dropped open.

"What . . . how . . . don't you get—lonely?"

The man cackled a dry, coughing laugh. "No. We have our books. We have our stories."

"What do you eat? I mean . . . how do you get food?"

"We go down. In the very dark middle of the night. And we bring back. What we need. The Admiral leaves us alone. And we leave him alone."

"Oh. Okay."

The librarian pulled a book from the shelf and pressed it into Jonathan's hands.

"Here. Start. With this one."

Jonathan looked down. The book was thick, with a red, pictureless cover. In plain gold script on the cover was the title: *Robinson Crusoe*.

"It's about getting stuck. On an island." The librarian winked at him. "With bloodthirsty natives."

"Uh. Thanks."

The old man just nodded.

As they walked back toward the door, the man stooped down to pick up a large cat off a chair. He held it in one arm and stroked it with his other.

"Read it. Bring it back. When you're done. And then you can have another. Book." He patted Jonathan on the shoulder and left his wrinkled hand resting there. "We'll be here."

"Okay. You and your cat?"

"No. Me and Ninety-Nine, here." The old man smiled and held the cat out toward him.

"Right," Jonathan said, reaching out to pet the cat. "You and your c—" Jonathan gasped and jerked his hand back. The animal he'd been reaching out to pet was not a cat at all. It was a rat. A beady-eyed, pink-tailed, black-coated rat that was bigger than most cats he'd seen. Its eyes glittered up at him above two huge top front teeth that poked sharply out of its mouth.

"God! It's a rat! It's huge!"

The librarian laughed, a deeper laugh than before. His eyes closed when he laughed.

"Yes. Yes," he giggled and stroked the rat gently from its head to its naked, ringed tail. "My big, beautiful boy. Ninety-Nine. Is his name."

"That's the biggest rat I've ever seen. By a long shot." Jonathan was backing toward the door.

The librarian giggled again and nodded. "Yes. Very big. Years and years. It took me. A lifetime. Always bigger." The monstrous rat leaned back into the librarian's scratching fingers.

"You . . . made him that big? How?"

"Oh, time. Patience. Attention. Years. I found the very biggest. Rats. One boy. One girl. And I put them together." The rat's tail curled lovingly around his arm. "I let the babies grow. Just a little. To find the biggest. And I let the others go. After I cut off their tails."

"You cut off their tails?"

Another smile spread across the librarian's lined face. "Of course. So I would know. Who they were. Brothers and sisters can't make babies. You know. And I would find another. Big one. *With* a tail. And make more babies. And again. And again. So many times. So many tails. And always bigger." A cloud passed over the old man's face, erasing his smile. "I almost lost it all. With Seventy-Six. She wouldn't. Have babies. *Couldn't*, I was afraid." His smile returned and the cloud lifted. "But then she did. And they were beautiful. And big."

Goose bumps rose on Jonathan's arms.

"You mean—this is your *ninety-ninth* rat?"

"Oh, no," the man chuckled. "Much more. Than that. I just stopped. Counting. One Hundred sounds so ugly. It's no kind of name. For a beautiful rat."

"Oh. Right." Jonathan put his hand on the doorknob and turned it.

"You'll come back? To us? And another book?"

"Yeah. Sure," he answered, opening the door to the inky blackness of the passageway.

"We hope so. How are things going? Out there?" The librarian's white eyebrows cocked out at the darkness looming past the doorway.

Jonathan licked his lips. He smelled lightning, saw bodies in a freezer, heard a monster rattling an iron door and a bully taking control.

"Fine, I guess."

"Oh. Well." The librarian sighed again, wearily. "It never stays fine. For long. Things always go bad. Out there. So much evil. And darkness. And so much more always coming. That is why we stay here. Keep your wits. About you."

Jonathan eyed the waiting corridor. At the edges of the light, furry shadows scrambled and hid. He wondered how many of them were missing tails. He licked his lips.

"Can I borrow a candle?"

CHAPTER TWELVE
"I KNOW WHAT YOU DID"

When Jonathan got back to the light and the world and the rest of the Scars, Sebastian was sitting in the Admiral's chair with his feet up on the table. In his hands was the Admiral's sword. The very one the Admiral had been holding high in the storm, the one that had brought down lightning and death for himself and all of the grown-ups (except one).

Most of the boys were hanging out in the dining room. Some were munching on great mouthfuls of food. A few had found a deck of cards and were playing at a table. Most were just sitting around or lying around or standing and looking out the windows into the courtyard, which was once again dripping with a drizzling rain.

Benny, Roger, Gregory, and some other kids were seated around Sebastian, looking eagerly to their leader's smirking face like baby birds hoping for a worm.

"Hey! Johnny! Come here," Sebastian called when he saw Jonathan enter the room with his candle in one hand and the book tucked under his arm. Walter and Colin had jumped up when they saw him and they followed him to Sebastian's table, their eyes full of questions.

There were crumpled-up candy wrappers on the table and little dark smears of chocolate in the corners of Sebastian's mouth. He licked at them like a cat. Sebastian looked Jonathan up and down with a frown.

"Where'd you get that book?"

Jonathan shrugged.

"Found it."

Sebastian sniffed and picked at something between his teeth.

"We're divying up the grown-up's rooms," he said. "I got dibs on the Admiral's. But there's four more. Which one do you want?"

Jonathan looked around at the other boys. Their eyes were wide, waiting. Benny's reptilian eyes were narrow, glaring.

"Five? There's sixteen of us. Why would I get one?"

Sebastian frowned and shrugged.

"Whatever. Maybe I like you. Who cares. Don't you want one? Or do you want to keep sleeping in your little cell?"

Jonathan eyed the other kids. There were seven, counting Benny, waiting on his answer. Most of the kids were older—and bigger—than he was.

"Uh, no, thanks. Someone else can have it, I guess."

Sebastian screwed up one eye thoughtfully, then scowled and snorted.

"Fine. Whatever. Suit yourself. I'll give it to someone else."

"Maybe we thould take turnth in the roomth, Thebathtian. To be fair," Colin suggested.

Sebastian's eyes dropped into angry slits.

"Maybe you should *th*ut up, Colin."

Colin furrowed his brow and looked down at his feet. Jonathan turned to walk away.

"Hey! *They* said you went to look at the Hatch." Sebastian pointed with his chin at Walter and Colin.

"Yeah."

"So? What is it?" Sebastian's voice still wore its bitter coat of "who the hell cares," but there was a sharp edge of real curiosity to it.

"It's . . . it's . . ." Jonathan's voice faltered. He almost spilled it all, almost spit out everything about the eerie door with its ominous sounds and freezing spray and moss-covered skull.

But he stopped.

If he told them everything, they might want to see it for themselves. And if they went to see it, they might continue up the other staircase, and they might find the librarian. He didn't want them to. He wanted to keep the library a secret, just for himself. Like the key in his pocket. And the reason he was sent to Slabhenge in the first place.

"It's just a door," he said, with a shrug and a roll of his eyes.

"A door?"

"Yeah, like an old metal door. It's locked, though." He shrugged again and turned to walk away. "No big deal."

Walter and Colin followed at his elbow as he walked away into the kitchen. He was starving. Once they were away from Sebastian's ears and safe in the empty kitchen, they peppered him with questions.

"Where were you, man?"

"What took you tho long?"

"We waited for you at the top of the stairs! Where did you go?"

Jonathan looked around and grabbed the end of a loaf of bread someone had left sitting out. He took a big bite and gnawed it on one side of his mouth.

"I got lost," he answered with a shrug. "Went the wrong way."

"Where'th your lantern? What'th with the candle?"

Jonathan shrugged again and looked away.

"I broke my lantern. Then I found this. No biggie. What have you guys been up to?"

Walter rolled his eyes. "King Sebastian out there is really living it up. He's claimed the Admiral's room, of course, and most of the best food. He's called some big meeting in a few minutes, before dinner. I don't like that guy, man."

Jonathan grabbed an apple that was sitting on the counter and bit into it.

"You thould have thaid yeth to the room, Jonathan."

Jonathan crunched an especially big bite and chewed it loudly.

"What? Why?"

Colin sighed and scratched at his arm.

"Becauth. Now Thebathtian ith mad at you."

"Why would he be mad? I said no to be nice."

Colin shrugged. "He gave you a room. It wathn't to be nithe. It wath to thow that he'th the bawth. You made him look bad."

"I did not!"

Colin looked up at Jonathan with worried eyes.

"I don't think that'th how he theeth it." Behind them, through the door, Sebastian hollered for everyone to gather for the meeting. Colin pinched at his neck and started for the door with his pigeon-toed walk. "He'th only the king if we let him be. And you didn't let him."

Jonathan swallowed his apple and gave Walter a questioning look. Walter shrugged.

"The kid's weird. But he's smart, you know?"

"Yeah. I think he is."

In the dining room, Sebastian was sitting on a table, the blade of the Admiral's sword resting on his shoulder.

"All right, boys," he said to the last few boys grabbing chairs or a spot on the floor. "Time to get some stuff squared away. Some of us are taking the rooms upstairs. The rest of you can sleep wherever you want. Whenever you want. There's no all-dark tonight." There was a low murmur of approval from the group.

"We're gonna meet together every day," Sebastian continued. "Like, every night and every morning. To make sure everything's still fine. We'll meet right here."

"Every day? But . . . when are we going to inform the

authorities?" Francis asked. "You said this was just for a couple of days, Sebastian."

Sebastian tucked the chocolate-stained corners of his mouth down. "Yeah. Or whatever. We'll see. There's no rush." Benny jumped up and hissed something in Sebastian's ear.

"Oh," he said. "This is important. Did anyone find a key lying around?"

No one answered. Jonathan's mouth went dry and he fingered the Admiral's key through his pocket.

"We can't find the key to the Admiral's office," Sebastian went on. "Benny says the Admiral always carried it with him, but I—checked, and he doesn't, uh, have it. And the door is too big to break down." Jonathan thought of his one time in the Admiral's dark office. He remembered the smell of alcohol and the papers and files that the Admiral had, the papers that held the secrets of the crimes the boys had committed to get sent to Slabhenge. His grip on the key tightened through the fabric.

"Why do you need to get in there?" Miguel asked.

Sebastian shrugged. "There's paperwork and stuff that Benny wants. Plus, a bunch more of the Admiral's chocolates. And"—Sebastian smiled and cocked his eyebrows—"the Admiral's booze, of course. That could be fun." Some of the boys giggled nervously. "Well, if you find an old key, hand it over. It's around here somewhere. Whoever finds it gets a room upstairs and a handful of chocolates."

Sebastian rose to his feet and pointed with the sword toward the kitchen. "Meeting's over. You know where the food is. Dinnertime is whenever you're hungry. Same with breakfast. Any questions?"

"What can we eat for dinner?" another kid asked.

"Whatever you want."

"What are we doing tomorrow?"

Sebastian shook his head in exasperation.

"Whatever you want," he repeated impatiently. "Look, no more questions. Do what you want. That's the point. *They're* not here anymore. *We* are. It's us. Just us. The Scars."

"We *thould* have thome ruleth."

Sebastian clenched his fists and gritted his teeth.

"We don't need any rules," he seethed. "We don't *want* any rules." He held his hands out to the group. "Do we?"

There were some shaking heads, some grumbles of agreement, a few loud shouts of *no!*

"What about food?" Colin persisted.

"What about it?"

"If we all jutht eat whatever we want, we'll run out. We need to plan it out."

Sebastian smoldered like a dynamite wick. He opened his mouth to spit out an answer, but Jonathan beat him to it.

"He's right, Sebastian. The Admiral probably didn't order enough food for us all to eat like this. We're gonna run out."

Sebastian's eyes clouded with doubt. His dynamite wick sputtered. He licked his lips.

"Well . . . fine, then. We should—be careful about eating too much, I guess. Don't go crazy. Hell . . . go back to eating oatmeal if you want. But I've eaten enough oatmeal." He popped another square of chocolate into his mouth and chewed it loudly to make his point. Benny murmured something to him and he grinned a sticky brown smile. "And the supply boat comes in two days. Then we'll have plenty of food."

A thought shot into Jonathan's head.

"What about the mail boat?" he asked.

"The mail boat, *Johnny*, comes every day."

"So it'll come tomorrow?"

"Yeah. So?"

Jonathan looked around. He didn't want to make Sebastian look bad in front of the group.

"Well . . . so . . . we'll need something to give to it, right? Wouldn't it be suspicious if we didn't?"

Sebastian stopped chewing with his mouth stuck open.

"Oh," he said after a moment. "Yeah. Right. I was gonna get to that." He chewed thoughtfully for a few seconds before continuing. "We all still need to write letters every day, just like we were. No one eats dinner until we have your letter." Benny jumped up again and whispered something to him. Sebastian nodded. "And I'm reading every one. No one says anything about the grown-ups or the lightning or anything. Everything's just A-okay here at Slabhenge, right? Walter, go grab a bunch of paper and pens."

They all sat in silence, writing their letters home.

Jonathan stalled, looking around at the other boys bent over their papers. Tongues poked out of mouths. Eyebrows crinkled. Pen tips scratched on paper. Out through the windows, the sky was darkening toward night. It was raining hard now, the afternoon's drizzle turned to a steady pour. The boys around him were squinting to see their own words.

When each boy finished, he walked up and handed it to Benny, who read it over. He'd nod and hand it back and the boy would address the envelope and it would go in the mailbag.

Jonathan stared at his blank sheet of paper, trying to find words in the darkness. Colin sat beside him. He'd already handed in his letter, but he'd gotten another piece of paper and his hands were fluttering busily around it.

"What are you doing?" Jonathan asked him in a whisper.

"Origami," Colin answered. He made a few more quick folds and then held up the paper, now folded into an intricate shape. "Thee? It'th a bird. A crane." His smile rose and then flitted away. He handed the paper bird to Jonathan.

"Cool. Thanks. Where'd you learn to do that?"

Colin shrugged. "I thtole a book." They grinned at each other. Jonathan took a breath and went back to his own blank piece of paper.

Benny sneered at Jonathan when he walked up with his letter. He was by himself at the end of a long table, a tall white candle lighting his face. His eyes skimmed over Jonathan's letter.

"Looks good enough, Johnny. I guess. Who's Sophia?" His eyes flashed up to Jonathan. In the candlelight, they looked hungry and black, like a cobra's. But less honest.

"She's . . . a friend."

A venomous smile rose like oil at the corners of Benny's mouth. The points of his teeth showed like fangs. He lowered his voice to a taunting hiss so the boys at the other tables couldn't hear.

"No, she's not. I saw your paperwork, Johnny. In the Admiral's office, the day you got here." His foul smile widened. Jonathan's breaths got shallow and fast. His mouth went dry. *"I know what you did. I know. You better do everything Sebastian says. And everything I say. Or I'll tell. And you don't want me to tell, do you?"*

Jonathan shook his head, one small shake side to side.

Benny grinned. He handed Jonathan an envelope. When he spoke, his voice was loud again.

"Here you go, Johnny. Write Mommy and Daddy's address right there." He flashed a smile like a knife blade in the dark and turned back to his own letter.

Jonathan had to steady his shaking hand to write down his parents' address. The librarian's warning echoed in his mind: *Things always go bad. Out there.*

CHAPTER THIRTEEN
THE THECRET

Colin was right about Sebastian being angry at Jonathan. He showed his anger after dinner, in the flickering light of a dozen candles scattered throughout the dining room.

Sebastian swallowed a final bite of a shortbread and wiped the corners of his mouth, then stood up. He banged his metal plate on the table to get everyone's attention.

"All right. In the morning, we'll have to meet the mail boat again. You ready for that, Gerald?"

Gerald burped and nodded.

"Good. You all can drag your mattresses wherever. Even in here, if you want." The boys looked around. It was a big room, with plenty of floor space. But it was also a little close to the freezer.

"Now," Sebastian continued, "it's time to refill the coal furnace. We need two people. How about . . ."—his voice trailed off as he scanned the room—"Colin. And . . . let's see." His dark eyes glittered in the candlelight and flashed to Jonathan. He smiled. "Johnny. Oh, wait . . . you don't like fire, right?" Jonathan's eyes dropped to the floor. He rubbed his hands on his sleeves. "Well, sorry. Everyone has to take a turn. Be sure to fill it real full."

Sebastian grabbed a candle and stalked away with Benny and some others at his heels. They disappeared out the door that led up to the grown-ups' bedrooms.

Colin sighed and looked at Jonathan.

"Well," he said, "I geth we thould jutht go and get it over with. It'th not that bad."

Jonathan nodded. "Yeah. Okay. Let's do it."

The furnace was in a room beneath the kitchen, down a steep, short staircase. The room was hot and muggy and smelled like a wet ashtray. The ceiling was so low, Jonathan could have jumped and touched it. It, too, was made of stone blocks, held together with crumbling mortar and forming a steep arch, so that it curved down to meet the floor at both side walls. The furnace was a black iron monster the size of a car, squatting in the far darkness. It hissed and hummed and rumbled. The rest of the room was filled with waist-high heaps of lumpy black coal. A little trail wound between the coal piles to the furnace.

"That's a lot of coal," Jonathan said.

"Yeah," Colin answered, hanging his lantern from a hook on the ceiling. "Coal delivery day ith the wortht. Three hourth of wheelbarrow work. And for every little lump you drop, you get a minute on the Thinner'th Thorrow. I dropped ten latht time."

"Ouch."

They walked to where a couple of shovels were leaning against a wheelbarrow. They each grabbed one and started scooping coal into the wheelbarrow. The scraping of their shovels echoed on the low stone ceiling. Black dust from the coal sifted up and soon they were both coughing and clearing their throats as they shoveled.

"What wath really there?" Colin asked between breaths. "At the Hatch?"

"Just a door," Jonathan panted back. "I told you."

Colin shook his head. "You're keeping thomething. A thecret."

Jonathan stopped and leaned on his shovel. "How do you know that?"

Colin shrugged and kept on shoveling. "I watch. Clothely. And lithen. Almotht no one elth doth that. And I can tell you didn't tell everything."

Jonathan sighed and scraped another shovelful of coal into the wheelbarrow.

"You're good," he admitted, then told Colin about the sounds and the skull and the strange, ancient-looking door with the spinning handle. He didn't mention, though, the other staircase, or the librarian.

"A thkull. That'th tho weird. It'th like a . . . warning. Or a threat." He dropped his shovel and grabbed the handles of the full wheelbarrow. Maneuvering through the coal piles, he rolled it up to the growling furnace. Jonathan followed cautiously behind him.

At the furnace, Colin stepped forward and turned a few rusty bolts, then swung open a thick metal door. A blast of heat rippled out into the room. Jonathan took a step back and covered his face with one arm. He squinted out from under his elbow.

Inside the furnace was a burning hell of flames and fire, glowing in shifting hues of red and orange and blazing white. He couldn't look at it without narrowing his eyes to slits. The heat made the air waver and ripple.

Colin turned and saw Jonathan backing away. He blinked and then swung the furnace door mostly closed.

"You're thcared," he said, and Jonathan looked away. "Why?"

Jonathan just shook his head. Sweat beaded on his forehead and dripped down his face.

"You can trutht me," Colin said. His voice was soft, but insistent. Jonathan nodded and swallowed a ball of fear.

"Something . . . happened," he said, his voice shaky. "To me."

"What?"

Jonathan took two steps forward and undid the buttons on the sleeves of his shirt. One after the other, he pulled his sleeves up to his elbows and held out his arms to Colin.

Colin's coal-smeared face leaned closer to see. The lantern swung from its hook above them, making shadows writhe and twist around them. His eyebrows rose into the beads of sweat on his forehead. His mouth rounded in surprise.

He reached out and ran his fingers softly over the twisted grooves etched into Jonathan's skin. He brushed his fingernails gingerly over the toughened swirls of hard scar tissue that covered Jonathan's arms all the way from his wrists until they disappeared into his bunched-up sleeves. Jonathan's hands were shaking. With a gasp he pulled back suddenly and tugged his sleeves back down to cover his tortured arms.

"I . . . I don't like to show people," he stammered, desperately fumbling with his sleeve buttons. "I don't like to see them myself," he added more quietly. Colin grabbed Jonathan's trembling hands and held them still. Then he gently buttoned up the first of Jonathan's sleeves.

"They're burnth," he whispered. "Were you caught in a fire?"

"No." Jonathan shook his head. Tears sprang to his eyes and he looked away. "I was not in the fire."

Colin finished buttoning the second sleeve and looked up at Jonathan with eyes that were quiet and wide. He was watching. Closely. And listening.

"When? When did thith happen?"

Jonathan took a ragged breath. "A while back," he answered.

"What happened?"

Jonathan ground his teeth together. He blinked and shook his head.

"We should—finish the coal."

"Okay. Thure."

Colin turned and reopened the furnace door. The small, suffocating room once again filled with heat and angry light. Colin pushed the wheelbarrow right up to the furnace's open, red mouth.

"It'th okay," he called back over his shoulder. "I think I can do it mythelf." He grabbed both handles of the wheelbarrow and struggled to tilt it up into the furnace. He grunted and his feet slid and slipped on the coal-dusted floor.

Jonathan shook his head and winced. He watched Colin wrestling with the heavy wheelbarrow. His arms were crossed, the fingers of each hand rubbing through his sleeves at the burns on his arms. Colin looked so small, so helpless by the burning fire. So in need of help. Jonathan stepped forward, shoulder to shoulder with Colin, and took hold of one of the handles. Together they lifted it and dumped the load of coal into the waiting flames. There was a shower of sparks and a fresh wave of heat. Jonathan's arms burned. They let the wheelbarrow drop and Colin slammed the furnace door.

The boys stood panting, leaning on the wheelbarrow. Their hands were black, and sweat dripped muddy trails through the coal on their faces.

"Well," Jonathan said, pulling at his shirt where it stuck to the sweat on his body. "That wasn't so bad."

"Yeah," Colin responded between coughs. "That wath one. It taketh five to fill it."

Walter and Colin and Jonathan pulled their mattresses into a corner of the dining room by the kitchen, away from the windows to the courtyard, which let in moonlight and cold drafts and memories of lightning.

Other groups of boys had their mattresses together in clumps, too, here and there around the room. No one wanted to sleep alone.

They laid their mattresses like spokes on a wheel so their heads could be together. They'd each carried a candle when they'd gone together to the old sleeping quarters to claim their beds, and when they lay down, they put the three candles together on the floor in the space between them. Their faces were smooth in the candlelight, their hair dark, with cold blackness all around.

Walter lay on his stomach, watching the candle flames. Colin was on his elbows, quietly folding more paper animals. Jonathan opened the book the librarian had given him. The pages were yellow and fragile and they whispered in the quiet of the room when he turned them.

"What book is that?" Walter asked. Jonathan turned back to the cover.

"*Robinson Crusoe*," Jonathan read. "*By Daniel Defoe.*"

"I've heard of that," Colin said.

"Is it any good?" Walter asked.

Jonathan shrugged.

"I haven't started it yet."

"Could you?"

"I was going to."

"No, man. I mean, like, out loud?"

"Oh. Um, yeah, I guess. If you want." He licked his lips and cleared his throat and paged back to the first line. "*I was born in the Year 1632, in the City of York, of a good Family, tho' not of that Country, my Father being a Foreigner of Bremen, who settled first at Hull,*" Jonathan began. Reading was hard in the dim, flickering light; he followed the words he read with a fingertip.

"York? Like New York?" Walter asked.

"No. I think it meanth York in England," Colin explained.

"Oh."

Jonathan continued. "*He got a good Estate by Merchandise, and leaving off his Trade, lived afterward at York, from whence he had married my Mother, whose Relations were named Robinson, a very good Family in that Country, and from whom I was called Robinson Kreutznaer.*"

"I don't get it," Walter complained.

"It's an old book," Jonathan said. "It's written all kind of old-fashioned. Nothing important has happened yet, though, I don't think."

"Oh. Okay."

"And stop interrupting."

"Okay."

"*But by the usual Corruption of Words in England, we are now called, nay we call our selves, and write our Name, Crusoe, and so my Companions always call'd me.*"

"What is that?" a voice asked over Jonathan's shoulder. He craned his neck to see Miguel standing in the shadows, the candlelight playing on his curious face.

"Just a book. *Robinson Crusoe.*"

"You gonna read that whole thing?"

"I don't know. I'm gonna start, at least."

"Huh." Miguel stood in the darkness and hugged his shivering body.

"Do you—uh—wanna listen?" Jonathan asked.

"No," Miguel answered quickly. "But, whatever. I'll go grab my mattress."

A moment later, Miguel reappeared with another boy, both dragging their mattresses behind them. Walter and Jonathan and Colin spread theirs apart to make room.

"I'll start over," Jonathan said when everyone was settled in. "*He got a good Estate by Merchandise, and leaving off his Trade, lived afterward at York, from whence he had married my Mother—*"

"Can I listen, too?" Tony stood just outside the circle of light, a pillow under his arm.

"And me?" another voice asked. Jonathan looked up and saw David standing there.

"Sure."

The boys already there made room in the circle for two more. Soon, there were seven heads facing one another through the flames.

"I'll start over," Jonathan said again with a sigh.

And he did, with six pairs of ears listening to his whispered words. They all listened together to the story of a man trapped on an island, far from his family. The story held them together like the light from their candles, warm and close against the dark stone and shadows.

But out in the darkness that surrounded them, there was the scurrying of rats. And above them, he knew, Sebastian slept with a sharp sword in the Admiral's bed. And below them, a hungry menace knocked at an ancient door. And even then, surrounded by friendly faces, his dark fears whispered at him, and the flickering warmth of their candles' light seemed terribly small and fragile.

Dear Mother and Father,

I am still here at Slabhenge. Of course. The food has gotten even better. I hope that you are doing better. Give my love to Sophia.

Jonathan

CHAPTER FOURTEEN
CRIMES MUST BE PUNISHED

The mail drop went off without a hitch the next day.

Crusty old Cyrus was there instead of Patrick, and he didn't even bother talking to "Mr. Vander." The bags were traded without a word and the boat motored off into the waves and fog and was gone. The rest of the boys, who had been hiding safely around the corner, came out to peer through the arch at the disappearing boat. It looked so small, and the distance so great. A gust of wind blew a mist of salty spray into their faces.

"One more day," Sebastian said with satisfaction. "At least one more day." He held the Admiral's sword casually in one hand, its blade resting against one of his cheeks. "Hand out the mail, Benny," he said, before spinning and heading back across the courtyard.

Benny pulled the rumpled envelopes out of the mailbag one by one and called out the names written on them. Jonathan jumped when his own name was called.

"Grisby. Got one for you here, Johnny." Jonathan bit his lip and stepped forward to claim his letter. Benny held it out and Jonathan grabbed it, but Benny didn't let it go right away. Jonathan looked up at him and tugged a little harder, and Benny narrowed his eyes and smirked. "I wonder what Mommy and Daddy have to say to you, Johnny," he said in a quiet voice. "Nothing too nice, I bet, huh? After what you did?" Jonathan's heart clenched like a kicked puppy and he felt the red creep of shame rising on his face. Benny showed his wet teeth and then let go. He blinked a bored, slow blink and called the next name.

Jonathan walked across the courtyard and inside. He lay down on his mattress, still with the others in the corner of the dining room, and ripped open the envelope. One folded piece of paper was inside. Jonathan swallowed, then pulled it open and read the words written in his mother's familiar, neat cursive writing.

Dear Jonathan,

Your father and I hope this letter finds you well. You were taken away just moments ago, and we've sat right down to write it. We will mail it tomorrow and hope that you will receive it soon.

The house feels so terribly empty now. We don't know what to say to you. So much needs to be said, we know, but we don't know what it is yet. We miss you. We've missed you for a long time now. We will write you every day, Jonathan, and hope that maybe we can find what it is that needs to be said. We go every day, with the flowers, like you asked. Maybe having you gone, for a while, will help all of us.

With love,
Your mother and father
p.s. If they let you write, please do

Jonathan chewed his tongue thoughtfully and read the letter again. He whispered a line aloud. *"The house feels so terribly empty now."* He licked his lips, then reread the last line. *"Maybe having you gone, for a while, will help all of us."* He blinked his eyes hard and sniffed.

A door slamming open behind him made him jump. He rubbed at his eyes quickly and stuffed the letter under his pillow.

Sebastian stormed into the dining room, dragging another boy by his collar. It was the little kid named James, whom Jonathan didn't know well, but he knew he was one of the boys to whom Sebastian had given one of the grown-ups' rooms.

"Everybody gather around!" Sebastian hollered. Benny and Gerald were just walking in from the courtyard. Sebastian pointed at them with the sword. "Get everyone in here," he commanded.

Jonathan jumped up and joined the nervous crowd

assembling around Sebastian and a terrified-looking James. They kept a few safe paces back.

"I wanted you all to see this," Sebastian said, glowering around at the group. "I just caught James here, sneaking into my room."

"It'th not really *your* room," Colin murmured.

"Shut up, Colin." Sebastian's eyes flashed cold fire at Colin, standing beside Jonathan. "I caught him in *my* room, going through *my* stuff."

"I'm sorry, Sebastian, I didn't think—" James whined, but Sebastian cut him off.

"Shut up, James. I caught him red-handed, eating my chocolate."

"It'th not really *your* chocolate."

"Damn it, Colin, you better shut your mouth."

Jonathan nudged Colin sharply with his elbow.

"*Drop it, Colin*," he hissed out of the corner of his mouth. Colin sighed angrily.

Sebastian scanned the crowd, looking for defiance. All the eyes dropped to the floor when Sebastian's met them, except Jonathan's.

"What are you going to do?" Jonathan asked.

Sebastian's dark eyes flickered with uncertainty. He chewed his lower lip and looked doubtfully at James, still trembling in his grip.

Benny slipped forward in the hanging silence and hissed

something into Sebastian's ear. Sebastian's brow furrowed and he whispered something back. Benny leaned even closer and put a hand on Sebastian's arm, whispering fiercely into his ear again.

Sebastian nodded after a moment and then raised his chin to the group. He pointed the sword at Gregory and Roger.

"Bring in the Sinner's Sorrow," he commanded. A murmur ran through the crowd. The two boys exchanged a glance, then ducked out into the courtyard, where the Sinner's Sorrow had sat since that final, fateful Morning Muster.

"No, Thebathtian," Colin said.

"Ye*th*, Colin," Sebastian spat. "Even with us in charge, crimes must be punished."

"You don't have the right."

Sebastian's face contorted in fury. "I have the *sword*, Colin! What are you going to do?"

Colin looked desperately to Jonathan.

"Do thomething!" he pleaded.

Sebastian looked expectantly at Jonathan, but Jonathan was looking at Benny. Benny's mouth was set in a small, grim smile and he shook his head at Jonathan just one time.

"Jonathan!" Colin begged.

Jonathan eyed Benny for one more moment, then dropped his eyes to the floor and shook his head.

Gregory and Roger grunted in, tugging the dreaded Sinner's Sorrow between them. They dragged more than carried it, and when they'd managed to pull it close enough to Sebastian, they leaned against it, gasping. The raindrops dripping down the dark wood looked like blood in the cloud-darkened light seeping through the windows.

Sebastian shoved James roughly toward the dripping Sinner's Sorrow.

"How many pieces did you eat?"

James gulped and looked out at the other boys. Again, all the eyes dropped.

"Um, like, one or two, Sebastian, but I—"

"One or two?" Sebastian reached in his pocket and pulled out a handful of shiny gold wrappers. One by one he let them drop to the ground. "One. Two. Three. Four." He cocked an eyebrow and raised the sword to point it at James. "One minute per piece for stealing. And one minute per piece for lying to me. Eight minutes on the Sorrow." Tears pooled in James's eyes. His bottom lip began to quiver.

"The watch, Benny," Sebastian said, holding out his hand. Benny handed over a tarnished silver pocket watch. Sebastian looked out again at the gathered boys. "Who wants a room? One just became available. It's got a window and everything. Doesn't it, James?" James sniffled and nodded miserably. "Okay, who wants it?"

There was a tense moment of silence. Finally, the kid named Reggie raised his hand.

"I'll take it."

Sebastian smiled like a snake and tossed Reggie the watch.

"Keep him on there for eight minutes, Reggie. I'm getting lunch. Make sure he doesn't cheat and make sure he stays on the whole time. If he gets up, the clock starts over. Then the room's yours."

Reggie nodded and stepped hesitantly forward.

"Get on there, James," Sebastian said, lowering his sword and turning toward the kitchen.

"Wait." Colin's voice stopped Sebastian cold.

"Thith ithn't right. We never voted on thith."

The muscles in Sebastian's jaw rippled and he took two slow steps toward Colin.

"Mind your own business, Colin." Sebastian's eyes flickered over to Jonathan, then quickly back to Colin. "This is fair. He stole from me."

"You thaid there were no ruleth."

"Well, Colin, I guess there's at least one. Don't mess with me." He gave Colin a long, steady glare. "Next time you talk back to me, you get the Sorrow, too."

Sebastian stalked off toward the kitchen. The rest of the boys stood for a moment, awkwardly watching James kneel down reluctantly on the awful device.

"I'll start the clock," Reggie said quietly. When James whimpered and sniffled, Benny and a couple of other kids laughed. They spun some chairs around and settled in to watch James wiggle and moan. Jonathan swallowed down a sour sickness and turned away. Most of the other boys did, too. A few wandered outside or into the kitchen, their eyes held carefully away from James's torment.

Colin stood beside Jonathan, pale and frowning.

"Thith ithn't right," he repeated.

"Just leave it alone," Jonathan whispered. "It's not a big deal. If you stop pissing him off, you'll be fine."

Colin looked back over his shoulder at James shaking on the Sinner's Sorrow, and the three vultures watching him from their chairs.

"I don't think tho, Jonathan. I don't think tho."

CHAPTER FIFTEEN
A DROWNED DUNGEON

Jonathan shuffled through the pitch-black corridors, his eyes on the uneven floor before him and his ears listening for the skittering sound of rat claws on stone. He held a tall white candle in one hand. He gripped the candle tight, his palm sweaty. His body didn't like being that close to the hot flicker of a flame. Neither did his heart, for that matter. He steadied his shaking as best he could and pressed on through the darkness.

He ducked under the now-familiar rope gate and descended the stairs, pausing for only a second to listen at the narrow passage that dropped down to the Hatch. Then he climbed the other staircase and retraced his steps to the closed door of the library.

Again, light showed from beneath it. And, again, low humming sounded behind it. He took a breath and then knocked on the door. The humming stopped, and the door creaked open.

"Ah," the librarian said, with a raise of his bushy eyebrows. "It's you. Again. Come in."

Jonathan entered the lighted warmth of the library and let the door close behind him.

"Back for another book?"

"Um, no. Just to look, I guess."

"Are you reading? *Robinson Crusoe?*"

"Yeah. A bunch of us are. It's pretty good."

"Yes. It is." The librarian turned and walked back among the shelves. Jonathan followed, the candle still in his hand. He stepped quickly away when he saw the giant rat, Ninety-Nine, atop a shelf at his shoulder, sniffing and stretching toward him with his nose. The librarian saw and smiled.

"Oh. Don't mind him. He just wants. To be petted." The librarian reached back an arm, and the rat scrambled up it, his claws catching in the woolen sleeve, and curled up around the librarian's neck.

"What is the Hatch?" Jonathan asked abruptly. The Hatch—the sound of its violent knocking and sloshing, how deeply it lurked in the darkness of the prison like a shameful secret, with the skull standing silent guard—had haunted his thoughts since he'd left it.

"The Hatch? Ah. Yes. Quite a curiosity. Isn't it?"

"Yeah. It looks so . . . old. And it makes all these weird sounds."

The librarian smiled a strange, knowing smile and shook his head.

"It is old. But it does not make any sounds. No. It's what's behind it. That makes the noise."

"Well, what's behind it, then?"

The librarian pursed his lips and leaned forward, cocking one sideways eye at Jonathan. Ninety-Nine's beady eyes sparkled at him.

"The sea, my boy. It is. The sea itself. Behind that ancient door."

"The sea? How?"

The librarian heaved a heavy breath and walked over to the closest window, mostly blocked by standing books. He pulled one of the books down and peered through the space where it had been. The gray light shone through the old man's wispy white hair.

"The water," the librarian whispered, looking out at the storm-tossed waves. "It is rising." He cocked one eye back over his shoulder toward Jonathan. "Or the island is sinking. Both. I think." He looked out again through the gap at the sea. When he spoke this time, his voice was different. Faster, smoother, less labored.

"Years ago, back in the asylum days, the water was not so high. There was a beach around Slabhenge then. A smooth stretch of sand. With shells, and logs, and pools. We had a pier, even. Big enough for large boats to dock at. I would sit on the pier, sometimes, and fish. Watch the sun set. Or rise. Look off at the distant mainland and wonder. Of course, I was a boy then. So long ago."

Jonathan stepped to stand behind him. He stood on his toes to see the white-capped ocean.

"You . . . were here when you were a kid?"

The old man's eyes were trained far off in the distance. His voice was feathery and far away.

"Oh, yes. I was born here. My mother and father were

both . . . patients here. She was a madwoman. He, a lunatic. The asylum was my home. My school. My playground. The guards were my aunts and uncles. My friends. My tormentors, sometimes." He brought one wrinkled hand up to stroke the rat perching on his shoulder. The gigantic animal twisted and stretched so that the old man's fingers could scratch his itchy places.

"They offered to send me away to the high school on the mainland when I was old enough. The head warden, I mean. He was a kind enough man, I suppose. But I refused. It all seemed too terrifying. Leaving the island. The walls. The water. So I stayed."

The librarian sighed. It was a weary sigh, tired and breathy and covered in the dust of years.

"I became the librarian's assistant. I did my learning from these books. And my traveling. My living, really, right here in these pages. When the old man died, the warden let me take his place. Not long after that, my mother died. And my father. And I just . . . stayed. When the asylum closed, they allowed me to stay, to care for the facility. Run the lighthouse. Keep it all from falling apart. And when it reopened as a school, the Admiral kept me on."

"So you've *never* left the island? You've always been here?" The librarian was still turned away, toward the sea, but Jonathan could tell from the old man's voice when he answered that he was smiling.

"Oh, yes. Always. I have never once left this island. This

beautiful, crumbling island. Not once. And I never will. Never."

Jonathan took a breath and a step back. The rat turned on the librarian's shoulders and narrowed his eyes at Jonathan, his pointy front teeth showing.

"And . . . the Hatch?"

"Yes. The beach, foot by foot, year by year, went away. Swallowed. Then, in a storm, the pier was washed away. Behind the Hatch is a staircase that leads down to the very bottom floor. The cellar, if you will. During the asylum days, it was a sort of special prison for the most troublesome." He returned the book to the shelf and half turned to look up at Jonathan in his queer way. "A dungeon, you would proba-bly call it. My father was there, briefly. During his dark days. Eventually, as the water rose, it was too wet for people. There was standing water at high tide. It was a storeroom then. High shelves. Then the water got too high even for that. It filled the room, began to climb the stairs. During one bad storm, maybe, oh, twenty years ago, there was a surge and it came all the way up, up into the main floor. So many rats died that night." He scratched his yellow finger-nails through Ninety-Nine's fur and nuzzled the rat's neck with his face.

"So they installed the Hatch. That's an iron door, solid through. Nine inches thick, bolted into the stone with foot-long bolts. Sealed with cement and mortar and soldered steel. Strong enough, they say, to hold the sea back. And those sounds you hear? That is the sea, crashing and surging beneath us. Sucking at forgotten windows. Opening and closing submerged doors. Tossing old furniture around. Rattling old chains. Chewing at the foundations. And always, always, knocking at the door."

He closed his eyes and sighed and stroked his monstrous rat.

"The sea is in the dungeon. Seething, beneath us. But it doesn't want to stay there." The old man's eyes opened and focused on Jonathan's. "It wants the whole island. It wants it all. And someday. It will. Get it."

Jonathan's mouth was dry. He blinked. His mouth was stuck open.

"Now," the librarian said, taking a step and brushing past him. "What book would you like?"

"I'm, um, still reading the first one," Jonathan said, shaking his head. "I don't need another one just yet."

The librarian stooped down and Ninety-Nine crawled down his arm and onto a shelf. The old man looked back at Jonathan and shook his head and smiled a crooked smile.

"No. You can't leave a library. Without a book." He scanned the nearest shelf with a finger and one sideways eye. Jonathan stood where he was and watched the hunched old man creak along the shelf, muttering to himself and shaking his head.

"Ah. Yes. This one. Is appropriate." He pulled a thick volume off the shelf. "Another island story. About a boy. And a crazy sea captain. And treasure found." He held the book to his nose and closed his eyes and took a deep breath, then handed it to Jonathan.

Treasure Island, the cover said in plain black letters on red leather. *By Robert Louis Stevenson.*

"Thanks. I better get back."

"Yes," the librarian said, walking with Jonathan to the door. "You should. Thank the Admiral. For letting you come. It has been so long." Jonathan stepped out into the dark corridor, holding the candle before him. The librarian closed the door nearly all the way, so that only his mouth and one eye were visible in the crack. "And say hello. To the ocean. For me. When you go past. The Hatch."

The door closed, leaving Jonathan with his feeble flame and the sound of rats and, in the darkness ahead of him, a rattling door to a watery dungeon.

CHAPTER SIXTEEN
SORROW'S SINNER

"You know the drill," Sebastian decreed from where he sat on the table, his shoes on the Admiral's great chair. "No dinner until we have your letter. Get it done." He was bent over, focused on the tip of the sword he was holding. He was using it to carve something into the surface of the table.

The boys each filed by to grab a pen and sheet of paper from where Benny sat frowning officiously at them, coiled up in a chair. Already out the windows the sun had set on their second day alone on the island. The room and its long tables were lit here and there by flickering candles.

Jonathan sat and looked at his paper. He remembered his mother's words from the letter that still waited under his pillow. *So much needs to be said,* she'd written. *But we don't know what it is yet.* His fingers balled into fists. His tongue was pinched between tight teeth. He looked up and saw Colin watching him from across the table. His flitting, hummingbird smile came and went and he looked down at his own paper. All around was the sound of pen points on paper. A thin mile of ink, measured in words. *I love you*s and *I miss you*s and *can't wait to see you*s. Messages from naughty boys, sent home to worried mothers. Jonathan blew a breath out through his nose and picked up his pen and began to write.

He scratched out a message, writing quick without thinking too much. He signed his name in a hasty scrawl and walked over to where Benny sat waiting to check their letters.

Benny looked his letter over with his usual sneer and then snorted.

"You really think that'll make them feel any better?" he asked. Jonathan looked down and didn't answer. "Fine," Benny said and handed the letter back. "Now the envelope."

Jonathan addressed the envelope and sealed his letter inside and slipped it into the mailbag.

He saw, lost in the shadows along the far wall, the Sinner's Sorrow standing in darkness. He looked at the rest of the boys. Their heads were down, their eyes away, the dim candlelight glinting off the shiny moving metal of their pens. With a last glance at the group, Jonathan ducked away and over to the Sinner's Sorrow.

In the darkness, the wood was black. He ran his fingers along the top rail, worn smooth by countless sweaty, tortured hands. He bent to touch the biting edge of the sharp kneeling ridge. Outside, rain tapped on the windows. His throat tightened, and his eyes watered. His words would never make his parents feel better, he knew. Benny was right. With trembling fingertips he felt the burns on his arms through his sleeves.

Then he bent down and knelt on the punishing edge.

The pain was immediate, and familiar. He remembered the Admiral's words from that first night: *You have done terrible things, haven't you, Jonathan Grisby?* Jonathan clenched his teeth and nodded and let the growing pain sharpen and fill his brain. His breaths were tight and jerky.

The letter had brought back memories. Memories that Jonathan kept quiet and locked away, down where they couldn't drown him. He let the pain push them back down, let it flood them away. His breathing eased. His jaw clenched even harder. His eyes closed.

"What are you doing?" The whisper snapped his eyes open. Colin was standing beside him, his eyes concerned, one hand fluttering at his neck, the other holding a half-folded paper crane.

"Leave me alone," Jonathan whispered back in a shaky voice. He closed his eyes again.

"Thith ith crazy. Why are you on that?"

"Go away, Colin."

"You thouldn't let the otherth thee you. You thouldn't let Thebathtian thee you." A nervous hand tugged softly on Jonathan's shoulder.

"What are you tho thad about?"

Jonathan screwed his eyes shut tighter and bit his lip until it hurt as much as his screaming knees.

"Jonathan! Come on, get off it! You're gonna hurt yourthelf!"

"I know."

"What? What do you—" Their hissed conversation was interrupted by a commotion behind them, at the tables.

"Sebastian! Sebastian, come look at this!" Benny's voice was triumphant and angry. There was an ugly delight in it.

Jonathan opened his eyes and looked over. Colin was still looking at him, his pale eyebrows knit together in worry. Jonathan jumped up and brushed past him to join the scene at the tables.

"I just barely caught it!" Benny was saying. He was handing a crumpled letter to Sebastian, who had stalked over with the sword in his hand. "Look! Look at what he wrote in the fold on the back!"

The rest of the boys had jumped up and were crowding around, wide-eyed in the candlelight, a few steps back. One of the older boys, skinny with black, curly hair and a twitchy face, was standing at the table in front of Benny, eyes darting back and forth between Benny and Sebastian. Jason was his name, Jonathan remembered. Walter had said he'd been sent to Slabhenge for stealing cars. He was frowning and chewing at the inside of one of his cheeks. He was one of the ones who had joined Jonathan's group the night before, to listen to *Robinson Crusoe*.

Sebastian snatched the letter and turned it over. His eyes scanned the paper and then his lips tightened into a thin, angry line. He glared up at the black-haired kid.

"Really, Jason? You?"

The kid shrugged and looked down.

"Sorry, Sebastian." His voice was a little shaky but

resigned. He wasn't crying. His eyes slid back up to Sebastian's. "I hate it here. I wanna go home."

Sebastian shook his head. He looked like he was going to spit. He held the letter closer to his face and read aloud.

"*We're in trouble. All the grown-ups are gone. Please send help.*"

A whisper ran through the crowd.

Sebastian set the sword on the table and reached to pull a candle in a tall brass holder a little closer.

"We're not in trouble, Jason," he said, his voice cold and angry. "*You* are." He held the letter out so that its bottom corner dangled in the slowly dancing flame. It caught fire and the flames licked quickly up the letter, curling it and crackling. The light in the room grew brighter. Sebastian's face was washed in brighter shades of red and flickering orange. He held the letter as long as he could, until the hungry flames were right up to his hand, and then let it drop to the damp stone floor at his feet. He sucked on his fingers and looked at Jason.

"Mommy and Daddy can't help you." He picked up the sword and tilted his head back and looked down his nose at Jason. "We don't need their help. They're the ones who *sent* us here, man! Screw them! And you want to, what, go running back? So they can blame us for what happened and send us to some other craphole? And you wanna do that to *all* of us?"

"No. I just wanna go home. I'm sorry, Sebastian."

Sebastian shook his head. "Home? Home?" His face twisted, then darkened. "No," he snorted. "You're not sorry. But you're gonna be." He pointed with the sword to the shadows where Colin and Jonathan had just been. "Sinner's Sorrow. Twenty minutes."

The watching boys gasped. Jason's face went pale.

Jonathan's knees were still burning. And he'd spent only a couple of minutes on the Sinner's Sorrow.

"You can't do that! That'th too long," Colin protested.

"*Damn* it, Colin. I've warned you to shut up." Sebastian turned to face Colin squarely. His face was etched in hard lines of anger. His eyes bore black holes into Colin's. He pointed the sword at Jason. "He gets twenty." The sword swung until its point was inches from Colin's nose. "You get ten."

"You can't make me."

"The hell I can't."

"I won't."

"Really?" Sebastian's eyes roved wildly through the room. They found Jonathan, and his jaw clenched. His sword swung to point at Jonathan. "Then your little buddy Johnny gets twenty. Is that what you want?"

Colin looked back and forth between Sebastian and Jonathan. Jonathan's mouth went dry and he tried to shake his head, but his neck wouldn't move. Colin sniffed and pinched at his neck.

"Okay. I'll do the ten minuth."

Sebastian smiled. "I know you will. I'll be running the watch."

"No." Jonathan's voice finally croaked free of his throat. Sebastian's gaze swung to him. "I'll do it. I'll take the twenty."

Sebastian narrowed his eyes and shook his head.

"No. Not you. This is Colin's. And then he gets tonight's coal duty. And no dinner. Come on. Jason's first."

Jonathan took one look at Benny's hungry leer and swallowed his protests.

The windows showed pure night blackness when Colin and Jason limped up from the coal room. Sebastian and his favorites had already gone up to their rooms, and the only light in the dining room came from the three candles set on the floor in the middle of the circle of mattresses. Jonathan and the other boys were already in bed, lying awake and waiting.

Colin crawled into his bed with a little grunt. His face was smudged with black coal dust. Jason fell onto his own mattress and pulled the blanket over his face.

"Are you okay, Colin?" Walter asked in a hoarse whisper.

Colin was lying on his back with one arm thrown across his eyes.

"It wath bad," he answered. "But not ath bad ath it'th gonna get around here."

The other boys looked at one another through the wavering candlelight.

"Well," Colin said, "are you going to read the thtory, Jonathan?"

Jonathan bit his lip.

"Sure," he said, and opened the book to the page he'd bent down to mark his spot. "It's a new chapter, called 'I Travel Quite Across the Island.'" He took a breath and cleared his throat. The other boys rolled over onto their elbows to listen. The warmth of the candlelight caught their ready faces.

"I mentioned before that I had a great mind to see the whole island," he began to read, and if there was the drizzle of rain or the skittering of rats, the sounds were lost in the words of the story.

JONATHAN'S THIRD LETTER HOME

Dear Mom and Dad,

I got your letter. Thanks for sending it.

I have had time to think here. And there's a lot to think about. You do seem far away. Maybe distance is a good thing.

I don't know anything. I don't know what comes next.

But I know that I think about you. Kind of a lot, maybe.

I know you told me not to say sorry. You told me I wasn't allowed to say sorry anymore. For what happened to her. But I have to. It's all I can say. Over and over and over. Even if you don't want me to. I have to.

I'm sorry. I'm sorry. I'm sorry. I am so sorry. Please give my love to Sophia.

Your son,
Jonathan

CHAPTER SEVENTEEN
THE SINNER'S REVENGE

The next morning, a supply boat was scheduled to arrive, with mail and food and anything else the Admiral had ordered. Sebastian had them all drilled and practiced and ready to go, waiting by the gates nearly an hour before the boat was supposed to get there.

Gerald was standing ready in the dead Mr. Vander's uniform.

"Remember," Sebastian was saying to them. "This ain't no big deal. It was always us that unloaded all the stuff anyway. Mr. Vander's gonna just be standing a little farther back this time, is all. I'll do *all* the talking, if we have to do any. We do it quick, we do it quiet, and we get them out of here."

The boys all nodded, Jonathan included. He looked back over his shoulder. Across the courtyard, Benny stood by the closed doors that led to the dining room. Jason and Colin were locked inside. The key was in Sebastian's pocket.

"I don't trust either one of you," Sebastian had told them in front of the whole group that morning after breakfast. "And we can't have you doing something stupid and messing this up for everyone." The last Jonathan had seen of Colin, he was standing, pinching at his neck and frowning thoughtfully as he watched Sebastian stalk out into the courtyard, brandishing the Admiral's sword. He also had the Admiral's hat on his head. It was a new touch Sebastian had added that morning when he'd come down for breakfast. Either he had a huge head or the Admiral had had a small one. The hat fit him perfectly.

Jonathan squinted out over the green and white of the tossing waves. Somewhere, just beyond his eye's reach, was the real world. Waiting. He breathed in, then out, and shivered. He wasn't ready yet.

The mailbag was heavy over his shoulder. That was his job, to hand over their letters. Polite little lies scrawled in childish writing to keep their kidnapped ship afloat. In the bag was his own letter. And Jason's new one, written that morning with Benny peering over his shoulder. Everyone's letter was in the bag. Except Sebastian's. Jonathan had noticed that: Sebastian never wrote a letter.

"Hey! I hear it!" Tony called out, and everyone snapped to attention. They waited.

"Aw, no, you didn't," Miguel said.

"I did!" Tony repeated. "I still do! There it is!"

All the eyes followed his pointing finger.

The boat was bigger than Cyrus and Patrick's little mail boat. Its noise was a deeper one, more rumble than whine, more easily lost in the constant low roar of the waves clawing at Slabhenge's walls. It pushed through the waves instead of rising and falling and hopping between them.

Gerald jumped up on his stool in the shadows by the gate opening and pulled the long coat tighter around him.

"Okay, boys," Sebastian said. "Here we go."

The boat rolled up sideways to where the staircase

dropped into the depths. Sebastian and David ran down to the water's edge, and a bearded man puffing a pipe threw a rope to them. Sebastian tied it off to the metal ring and the man slid a long wooden ramp over the rail of the boat.

The two men in the boat began sliding bags, crates, and boxes down the ramp, where they were grabbed by a boy or two and dragged or carried up the stairs and through the gate into the courtyard.

The boat rocked in the waves, and the ramp knocked and jostled, but it was all done in a matter of minutes. When the last crate was being hauled up the stairs, the bearded man waved to the fake Mr. Vander to come down to the boat.

The boys still on the stairs looked at each other.

"What do you need?" Sebastian asked the man.

"What do you mean? I need someone to sign that the order was delivered, boy!" The man waved a clipboard up toward Gerald.

"Oh," Sebastian said, looking back at Gerald standing in the shadows. "I'll bring it to him," he added quickly, snatching the clipboard before the man could object. He dashed away up the stairs.

Jonathan watched him talking with Gerald in the darkened archway. The man was watching, too, a frown on his bushy face.

"Here," Jonathan said to distract him. He shrugged the mailbag off his shoulder and handed it up to the boatman. The boatman coughed and spit. He took the mailbag from

Jonathan's outstretched hands and disappeared over the boat's side for a moment, then reappeared with a different one.

"Here's your incoming," he growled, handing it to Jonathan. Sebastian ran back to the boat and handed over the clipboard.

"Mr. Vander signed it," he panted.

The man looked it over.

"All right. And what about the next one?"

"The next what?"

The man pulled the pipe out of his mouth and shot Sebastian a withering look.

"The next order, boy. I assume ye all will still be wanting to eat next week, aye?"

Sebastian looked desperately up at Gerald, then over to Jonathan. Jonathan's stomach twisted into a nervous tangle.

"Oh, yeah, about that," Jonathan said, licking his lips. "The Admiral's a little behind. He's kinda sick, see. Most of us are. Bad flu going around. He told us to tell you that he'll be sending you next week's order in the mail in a couple days."

The man squinted and looked back and forth between Jonathan and the overcoated figure in the gateway. He popped the pipe back into his mouth and blew out a few little clouds of thick smoke.

"All right. Tell him to see that he does, then. I ain't coming all the way out to this damned rock to ask him what he wants."

"Yes, sir."

With a grunt the man heaved on the ramp, and Jonathan and Sebastian helped him pull it back on board the boat. The boat's motor roared and gurgled and the boat throttled away through the waves toward the mainland. Sebastian and Jonathan stood shoulder to shoulder, watching it go.

"Nice save, Johnny," Sebastian said.

"No problem," Jonathan replied, hefting the new mailbag onto his shoulder. "And it's Jonathan."

They turned and walked up the stairs. The rest of the boys fell in behind them. In the courtyard, they swung the gate closed. The boat was already out of earshot, nothing more than a receding white-trailed dot in the green sea.

The shipment was piled just inside the gate. A few big burlap sacks of flour and oatmeal and rice. A dozen or so big crates, and some smaller boxes.

"Okay, everyone grab something," Sebastian ordered. He picked up the sword where he'd left it leaning against the wall. "We'll move everything into—"

"Sebastian! Sebastian!" It was Benny's frantic voice, screaming from across the courtyard. He was ramming the door to the dining room with one shoulder and calling back over the other. Sebastian sprinted across the courtyard with Jonathan, the rest of the boys following close behind.

"It's Colin!" Benny shouted as they ran up. "He's going nuts!"

They all crowded around the big windows that looked into the dining room.

Colin stood panting in the middle of the room, by the Sinner's Sorrow. In his hands he was holding the ax they used to chop the wood for the kitchen stove. Jonathan wasn't sure what he was doing until another boy gasped, "Look at the Sinner's Sorrow!"

The wooden monster was nearly in ruin. Its top rail was completely gone, smashed and shredded. The dreaded kneeling rail was almost as bad, torn up and splintered by the sharp blade of the ax. Jason stood in the distant doorway to the kitchen, peeking timidly out.

"Stop!" Sebastian shouted, his voice choked with fury.

Colin's sneaky smile came and went, and he raised the ax high above his head.

"Don't!" Sebastian roared, but the ax came rushing down and bit again into the Sorrow's bottom rail. Through the window they heard the heavy *thwock* as it hit home, taking another bite out of the dark wood.

Sebastian dug through his pockets and pulled out the ring of keys and fumbled with them, stepping to the door. Colin raised the ax and again brought it down.

"You're dead, Colin!" Sebastian screamed, jingling the keys and trying to find the right one. "Dead!"

The ax flashed again and with a final crack the kneeling rail split and broke in half. Colin dropped the ax and looked toward the window where they all stood watching. His smile flitted to and from his face, shadowy and sad.

Then Colin walked quickly over to the doorway that

led into the depths of Slabhenge's dark labyrinth. By the doorway sat an unlit lantern and a lumpy sack and the Admiral's fancy hat. He picked up the lantern and the sack, then pulled the hat onto his head and looked back over his shoulder.

"Stop!" Sebastian shouted, finally jamming the right key in the door and swinging it furiously open. But Colin just threw the sack over his shoulder, tossed a two-fingered salute at the crowd from the brim of the Admiral's hat, and disappeared through the doorway.

All the others came rushing in. Sebastian sprinted to the doorway but stopped at the edge of the windowless darkness.

"Come back, you little jerk!" he hollered into the hallway, but the only answer was his own hollowly echoing voice. His lungs were heaving. He wiped at the corners of his mouth with his arm. "Bring me a lantern," he barked over his shoulder.

"No," Jonathan said. "Let him go."

Sebastian spun around.

"Let him go?! Why?"

Jonathan shrugged, thinking fast.

"What's the point? Where's he gonna go? We're in a prison on an island."

Sebastian's top lip snarled like a lion about to roar. He shook his head again, furious breaths hissing through his nose. The Scars all waited in silence.

"Should I get a lantern?" Benny whined.

Sebastian's jaw clenched. He shook his head and spit angrily onto the floor. "Don't bother," he finally seethed. "There's nowhere for him to run. He's dead." He turned his face back to the doorway and shouted at the top of his lungs. "You hear that, Colin? You're dead! Have fun living with the rats!"

He turned back to the staring crowd. He raised the sword and pointed it at them all.

"No one helps him. No one feeds him. You do, you're out, too. He's dead to us. Got it?"

His angry glare scoured the group. No one said a word. His eyes stopped at Jonathan, a scary kind of mad shining in them. Jonathan didn't lower his gaze, but he didn't raise his voice, either.

"All right," Sebastian yelled. "Get to work. Bring all that stuff in here."

Without a word, they turned and walked outside to bring in the supplies.

They walked past the ruined Sinner's Sorrow on their way to the door. Every pair of eyes secretly raced over the wrecked and ravaged torture device.

"*Way to go, Colin*," Jonathan whispered under his breath.

CHAPTER EIGHTEEN
MOTHER'S DAY

Jonathan didn't dare go back to visit the library that day. If he was seen ducking off into the passageways, Sebastian would be sure to think that he was helping Colin.

Sebastian spent the rest of the morning sulking in his room or storming around the kitchen, chewing and slamming cupboard doors. With their leader so ill-tempered, all the boys laid low. Some played cards or hung out on the stairs watching the water, but the *Robinson Crusoe* group lay on their mattresses and listened to Jonathan read more of the story. By lunchtime, there was only a thin pinch of pages left of the book.

Jonathan was halfway through his peanut butter sandwich when a shadow fell across the table. He looked up to see Benny's sour face glowering at him.

"Sebastian wants to see you in his room," he said.

"Okay," Jonathan answered, taking another bite.

"Now," Benny said. Jonathan put his sandwich down and followed Benny up the passageway to the adults' rooms.

They walked past the door to the Admiral's office, still closed and locked. The next door in the hall stood open, and Benny led him through it.

Inside, Sebastian was lying on a huge, high bed. It was fancy and old-fashioned, with a tall pole at each corner and thick curtains that ran between them. All the curtains around the bed were pulled open and Sebastian lay propped up on a pile of pillows, watching a TV that was blaring on a little desk at the foot of the bed.

"Here he is," Benny announced proudly.

"Leave us alone, Benny," Sebastian said with a bored voice. Benny frowned and gave Jonathan a dirty look and then walked out, closing the door behind him.

Sebastian sat up and scowled at the TV.

"The reception sucks," he said. "You can't hardly see a thing."

Jonathan shifted uncomfortably from one foot to the other.

Sebastian blew out an impatient breath and slid off the bed. He sat down at the foot of the bed and clicked the TV off, then looked up at Jonathan.

"Where is he?" he asked.

Jonathan didn't have to ask who Sebastian was talking about.

"I don't know," he answered truthfully.

"You're his friend," Sebastian persisted. "And I know you've been creeping around this place."

"I don't know where he is," Jonathan repeated. "This place is huge. He never told me he was leaving."

"I want him back. I don't like him being out there. It's not . . . right. I'm supposed to be in charge, right? I'm supposed to be taking care of everybody. I should know where he is, right?" Sebastian's eyes were sharp and troubled.

Jonathan shrugged. "It's not your fault," he said at last. "He ran away. You didn't make him leave."

Sebastian looked away and nodded, then his eyebrows lowered and he looked back to Jonathan.

"If you do see him, would you tell me?"

Jonathan swallowed and looked away. He didn't answer.

Sebastian frowned and shook his head.

"It didn't have to be like this," he said. "We could be doing this together, you know."

Jonathan looked at him.

"Doing what?"

"Running this thing. Being in charge. You're smart. This was all *your* idea, remember. You didn't have to make me the bad guy."

"I didn't make you anything," Jonathan protested.

"Yeah?" Sebastian jumped to his feet. Jonathan took a step back. "Someone has to be the boss. Someone has to make it work. How else do you make everyone write a letter? How else do you make sure no one tells the boat guys? How else do you get people to feed the furnace? Huh? How do you make it all work otherwise?"

Jonathan didn't have an answer. "I don't know. But I don't want to be in charge. I just want . . . I just want . . ."

"What, Johnny? What do you want?"

Jonathan blinked hard and looked at the floor.

"I don't know. I don't know what I want. I don't want anything, I think. And that's the problem."

He could feel Sebastian still glaring at him, could hear his angry breathing.

"Why did you even suggest all this? Do you *like* it here?"

Jonathan shrugged and looked up into Sebastian's face.

"I don't like it out *there*," he replied. "I just didn't want to go back to—all that. Here I can just be . . . nothing."

Sebastian regarded him for a moment. Then he nodded one small nod.

"Yeah. I don't like it out there either."

They stood looking at each other for a second. Then Jonathan's eyes dropped away and Sebastian walked over to a low dresser. A basket full of the Admiral's chocolates was on top. All around it, and spilling onto the floor, were wadded-up empty gold wrappers.

Sebastian unwrapped a chocolate and popped it into his mouth.

"You want one?"

"No, thanks."

"They're almost gone, you know. The chocolates, I mean. And without the damned key, I can't get into the Admiral's office to get any more."

Jonathan looked up at him. "I'm glad we can't get in there," he said quietly.

Sebastian's brow furrowed. "Why?"

Jonathan didn't blink or hesitate. "Because our files are in there. All the lists of the bad things we've done. The bad things we are." His eyes dropped to the floor. "I like it better like this. We're just the Scars, together. Whatever we did out there doesn't matter." He looked at Sebastian. "If that door opens, we just become our crimes again."

For a moment, there was only the sound of Sebastian's noisy chewing. Then he asked a question, but his mouth was so full and sticky that Jonathan didn't understand it at first.

"What?"

Sebastian swallowed.

"I said, why are you so damned sad? I never seen a kid as sad-looking as you all the time."

Jonathan looked away, around the room, then over at the window. Through the thick glass, he could see gathering black storm clouds.

Instead of answering, he asked a question of his own.

"How come you never write a letter, Sebastian?"

There was no answer for a long time. The gold wrapper fell from Sebastian's hand and fluttered to the thick rug on the floor.

"Shut up, Johnny," he finally said. "Go on, get out of here."

Jonathan nodded and walked to the door. Sebastian followed him and stood in the doorway.

"It's funny," he said, just before he closed the door in Jonathan's face. "You wanna stay because here you get to be nothing. And I wanna stay because here I get to be *something*."

The door closed with a click, and Jonathan stood for a moment before finding his way back downstairs to join the others.

Jonathan's toes connected solidly with the ball, sending it bouncing across wet stone to Walter's waiting feet. The ball—an ancient leather soccer ball that someone had found in an old storeroom—was hard enough that it actually hurt a little to kick it. Walter loved it, though, and was always pleading with the other boys to come out and play soccer. Walter passed it back and forth between his feet a few times and then launched it to Jonathan.

It was almost dinnertime, and the sky was getting dark. The game Walter had tried to organize had been called off when the clouds started to sprinkle, and only Jonathan and Walter were left outside.

"How you think Colin's doing?" Walter asked.

Jonathan kicked the ball back to him.

"I don't know. Fine, probably. He's pretty smart."

"Pretty? That kid's *crazy* smart. He ain't, like, super tough, though, you know?"

Jonathan sighed.

"Yeah. I'm worried about him. He's, uh, not exactly the Slabhenge type."

Walter laughed.

"Slabhenge type? Is anybody? I mean, what's the 'Slabhenge type,' man?"

Jonathan pursed his lips thoughtfully. He thought of Miguel and his wicked grin. He thought of Tony, who always

159

cooked up something crazy in the kitchen and tried to get other kids to try it. He thought of Jason, a kid who supposedly stole cars but tried to slip a note to his mom because he just wanted to go home. He thought of quiet David, busted and sent here for fighting back. He thought of Walter, laughing and begging kids to come outside and play. He even thought of Sebastian, who acted so tough but who had noticed Jonathan's sadness and asked about it.

"I don't know," he answered. Then he grinned and looked toward the dining room. "Roger and Gregory, I guess," he said in a low voice. "And Benny. Benny's definitely the Slabhenge type."

Walter returned the grin.

"Oh, yeah. He fits right in here with the rats, don't he?"

The ball tumbled back and forth between them.

"You know, you've never asked me," Walter said.

"Asked you what?"

"You've never asked what we all ask. Why we're here. Don't you wanna know what I did?"

Jonathan rubbed at his nose with his sleeve. He looked up at the clouds, black like coal smoke.

"I don't know," he answered. "It's not my business." The words came out sounding ruder and harsher than Jonathan had meant.

There was a low rumble of thunder. That and the muffled thuds of their feet kicking leather were the only sounds.

"Okay," Jonathan finally said. "Why are you here?"

Walter smiled, his teeth shining whitely in the growing gloom.

"I thought you'd never ask!" He slapped his hands together. "Mother's Day, man."

"Mother's Day?"

"Yeah. Check this out. Around the corner from our place is this shop that sells all this little fancy stuff. You know, gloves and watches and hats and stuff. It's my mama's favorite store. She's in there, like, every day. And she's always going on about this purse that's in the window, right? One of a kind, it says, custom-made. This big ugly pink thing. And I know Mother's Day is coming up. I don't got any money, but I wanna get my mama something nice, you know? Now, there's no chance of me affording it. And no chance of me just sticking it under my shirt, either, 'cause Mrs. Swanson who owns the place always has her stink eye glued to me whenever I'm in there. So the night before Mother's Day, I break in."

Jonathan stopped the ball with his foot and held it.

"Seriously?"

"Seriously. There's this high window in the alley, way at the back of the store, and I get on a garbage can and crawl up through it. Soon as I hit the floor, though, this alarm goes off. Crazy loud. And I freak out. But I run up to the front and I grab that purse and run to the back door, but I hear voices outside. So I go back to the window I came in through, right? And I manage to jump up and start to climb through, but then I freeze, halfway out."

"Why?"

"Cops, man. I see their flashing lights at the end of the alley. Then I hear 'em. *Behind me.* In the store. And I'm sitting there, half out the window, with my rear end hanging in the store, and this ugly pink purse in my hands."

"Oh, man! Did they handcuff you and everything?"

Walter's smile stretched across his whole face.

"Nope. 'Cause they didn't even *catch* me, man!"

"What? You ran away?"

"Uh-uh." Walter shook his head. "I just hung there. And those cops walked all around that store with their flashlights. All they had to do was look up and they'd-a seen my scared butt dangling there in the air. But they never looked up, man. And nothing was broken. And the doors weren't busted or nothing. And the cash register was just sitting there, full. So they thought it was a false alarm. I hung there in that window for half an hour and then they left."

"No way."

"Yeah, man. That's the truth."

"Then . . . why are you here?"

Walter shrugged and his smile faded.

"I guess it wasn't, like, a super-smart crime. Seeing as how it was a one-of-a-kind purse from my mama's favorite store and everything. Next time she went in, she was showing it off, bragging about how I'd saved up all my allowances to buy it for her. Of course, Mrs. Swanson knew I'd never bought it. So that was that. And here I am." Walter shook his head, a small smile on his lips. "You shoulda seen her, though. The morning I gave it to her? You shoulda seen how happy and proud she was, man."

Jonathan kicked the ball to him.

"So that's my story, man. What's yours? Why you here?"

Above them, a bolt of lightning stabbed across the sky. A sharp crack of thunder rattled the windows to the dining room. They both looked up.

"Come on," Jonathan said. "Let's go grab dinner."

Over dinner the boys hardly spoke. Their letters were written in silence. Even Benny kept his snorting and gloating to a quiet minimum. Jonathan wrote his letter with a fast hand.

In bed, under the shifting light of the candles, he held the newest letter from his parents, the one that had arrived that morning on the supply boat. He breathed slow, even breaths, and read it again. When the other boys were ready, he opened *Robinson Crusoe* and began to read. He read to the very end, looking up from time to time into the ring of faces listening around the flames.

When he closed the finished book and blew out the candles, he went to sleep, with his parents' letter lying open on the pillow beside his head.

When he blinked his eyes awake in the morning, the letter was still lying by his head.

But it was folded into a perfect, delicate crane.

JONATHAN'S FOURTH LETTER HOME

Dear Mom and Dad,

I got your second letter today. Thanks. I do remember that trip to the beach. You're right. It was a great trip. Maybe that's why I try not to remember it. Good memories only make everything else feel worse.

You don't have to keep telling me you love me. I think I know it's true. But I wouldn't blame you if it wasn't. I wouldn't love me.

Everything is fine here. We had steak for dinner tonight. I overcooked mine, but it was still pretty good.

Do you think there will ever be a day that I don't think about it? Do you think there even should be?

I hope you are feeling better with me gone. I'm sure it helps to not have me around. Reminding you. Please give my love to Sophia.

Jonathan

CHAPTER NINETEEN
A HOME

With *Robinson Crusoe* tucked under one arm, Jonathan made his way quickly toward the library. His scrambled egg lunch sat uneasily in his stomach.

He knew his way well now. He didn't have to slow down or try to remember which way to go, and he could walk fast with the lantern held out in front of him. He saw more rats this time, probably because he could move so much faster. They didn't have a chance to get out of the way. They were very big. And he was sure he saw at least a couple, scrabbling and squeaking away, that didn't have tails.

He kept expecting to turn a corner and see Colin, but besides the rats, the way before him was vacant and still. Soon he was knocking on the door of the library, and the librarian was letting him in.

"Finished *Crusoe*. I see," the librarian said as the door closed.

"Yeah. Thanks." He handed the book over.

"Did you enjoy the book? Very much?"

Jonathan shrugged.

"Sure. We thought it was pretty cool, I guess. Boring in places. Big words."

"Yes. And you're here. For another book."

"Well, we still have *Treasure Island*. We'll start that tonight."

"Excellent. But you can't leave a library."

"Without a book," Jonathan finished. "I know."

The librarian looked at him with one twinkling eye and smiled.

"Yes. My thoughts. Exactly. Let me find a book. That you'll like."

Jonathan wandered off among the shelves, browsing through the books, casually reading the titles embossed on the spines. He almost cried out when he was surprised by Ninety-Nine, curled up on a folded blanket between two stacks of books on a shelf. The gigantic rodent yawned a toothy yawn and sniffed his long, whiskered nose up at Jonathan.

"You can pick him up. If you want to," the librarian said, peering over the shelf behind him.

"Oh. No, thanks." Jonathan moved farther along the shelves, leaving the rat to return to his nap. He stopped by one of the windows, mostly blocked by neatly lined books. The storm outside was growing fiercer by the hour, rattling the glass with rainy gusts of wind.

"Last time I was here, you said something," Jonathan began. "About—running a lighthouse, or something. What did you mean?"

"Just what I said." The librarian's voice was distracted, his eyes still scanning the shelves to find a book for Jonathan. "I used to run the lighthouse. Years ago."

"What lighthouse?"

"Ours. Slabhenge's. The island was first a lighthouse. Even before the asylum. Going way back. Hundreds of years. That is its true identity, really. Before all the tragedy. It still *has* the lighthouse. Unused, of course. For years and years, unused."

"Where is it?"

"At the top. Of the middle tower. The one above the warden's quarters. The Admiral's now, of course. Keep going up the stairs. And you'll find it. Dusty and in disrepair. I'm sure."

"And you were in charge of it?"

The librarian sighed.

"Oh, for a while. Not much to it. Wash the windows. Check the wood. Polish the mirrors." The librarian's voice quickened and smoothed out, just as it had when he'd been talking on Jonathan's previous visit. "It's very outdated. Not electric. A place for a fire. Giant mirrors to magnify and reflect the light. The mirrors spin by hand crank. Had to make sure those were oiled and ready. I only had to light it a couple of times, during big storms. Don't know if I ever saved any ships or not." He coughed a scratchy, jagged cough and then chuckled. "Probably still a stack of wood in the bin up there. Rotten, I'm sure, and dusty, like everything else on this island."

"Oh."

Jonathan read a few more book titles. Some of them were so worn with age that they were unreadable. Some weren't even in English.

"Can I ask you something?" Jonathan asked.

"Of course."

"Not to be . . . rude or anything, but . . . how come you talk so much easier when you talk about stuff from a long time ago?"

The librarian straightened up to look over the shelf at Jonathan.

"Do I?"

"Yeah. You normally talk kind of . . . slow. Like it's hard. But when you talk about, like, the old days, you smooth right out."

"Hmm." The librarian cocked his head even more sideways than usual. It was almost all the way to the side. His neck looked painfully twisted. "I don't know. I wasn't aware. That I did." His mouth screwed into a tight, thoughtful frown. "Well, the past is easier. It's done. It's there for me. To look at. I can live there. And know where I am."

His eyes drifted away from Jonathan, up toward the ceiling. As he spoke, they shifted slowly around the room and down to the floor at his feet. His voice got a little quieter with each limping sentence.

"It's the present. That is so hard. Working at it. Finding your way. Forward. Picking your path. Having to leave the past. Behind." His voice was barely a hoarse whisper. "It's so hard. Easier, I think, to stay in the past."

"What about the . . . future?"

The old man shrugged.

"I don't need a future. I have a past. Instead. You can really only have one. Or the other. I think. And I like my island."

"But it's a prison."

The librarian smiled. "It's a home."

Goose bumps broke out on Jonathan's neck. He tugged nervously at his sleeves.

The librarian's head slowly untwisted until it sat at a more natural angle. His voice rose back above a whisper.

"Here you go," he said, handing a book over the shelf to Jonathan. "This one. Is perfect. I think. One of our newest books."

Jonathan took the green-and-black book from the librarian's trembling hand.

"One of your newest ones?" he asked. The book looked like an antique.

"Yes. We got it. Just before the asylum closed. For good."

Jonathan traced the letters of the title on the cover.

"*Lord of the Flies*?"

"Mmm. Quite modern. That one. Also has an island. As a matter of fact. And a group. Of abandoned boys."

"Abandoned?"

"Mmm. Left to fend. For themselves."

Jonathan gulped and looked up at the librarian, then quickly away.

"Really."

"Yes. Doesn't go very well. I'm afraid."

Jonathan squeezed the book into the crook of his arm and picked up his lantern.

"Off?" asked the librarian. "So soon?"

"Yeah. They'll be wondering."

"Yes. I imagine."

Jonathan opened the door and stepped a foot into the corridor. He turned in the doorway and spoke one last question to the man's curved back.

"What's your name?"

"My name?"

"Yes. What's your name?"

The librarian turned with shuffling steps to face him. Ninety-Nine was nestled in the crook of his arm, leaning into the old man's scratching fingers. The old man blinked once, then twice. He closed one eye and reached up from the rat to scratch his own nose. His gray tongue licked his chapped, powdery lips, and then his hand dropped back to pet the rat once more.

"My name." The scratching slowed, and then stopped. "Why, I'm not sure." His voice was tinged with wonder, but not worry. He seemed only mildly curious. "It's been so long since anyone has called me anything at all. I used to be a son.

Then an assistant. An employee. A lighthouse keeper. A librarian. But now . . . well, I suppose I'm—nothing." He smiled, an unsteady, slightly troubled smile. "Ninety-Nine has a name. But it isn't really his. I suppose. He's just borrowing it. I guess you could call me that. Ninety-Nine. If you wanted."

Jonathan pursed his lips and held the book tighter to his body.

"No, thanks," he said. "I'll just call you sir, if that's all right."

The librarian smiled. The smile was as crooked as his hunched shoulders. "Of course. It is. Come back. Soon."

Jonathan hurried through the lightless hallways, the lantern swinging from his leading hand. He didn't slow to look down other halls for Colin. He was ready to be back to normal voices, to daylight and people.

He was almost jogging when he turned the last corner and stumbled, blinking, into the light of the dining room, so bright after the blackness of twisting stone and shadow.

"There he is!" he heard Sebastian's voice bark. He squinted and saw the older boy standing on a chair with the sword pointed right at him. "Grab him!"

CHAPTER TWENTY
THE FREAK AND THE RAT

Rough hands grabbed him by both arms and dragged him over to a chair in the middle of the dining room. Sebastian stood before him, his face white with anger. His eyes glittered like twin flames.

"Where were you, Johnny? His hideout?"

"What are you talking about?"

"What were you two doing? Giggling and shoving them in your mouth as fast as you could?"

Jonathan looked desperately around at the other faces. They all looked nervous. Walter held his hands up in a little shrug and crinkled his eyebrows sympathetically.

"I don't know what you're talking about, Sebastian, really—"

"Oh, cut the crap, Johnny. I know you were with him. Tell us where he is. Or it's gonna get ugly."

Jonathan opened his mouth to argue. Then closed it. He looked steadily into Sebastian's eyes. "What happened?"

"Like you don't know!"

Jonathan kept his voice calm. "What happened?"

"Fine. Let's all play a little game of pretend with Johnny." A rotten, ugly half smile rose to Sebastian's face. "We're all eating lunch. You, too. And somehow, while we're all down here, all the chocolates just—disappear! All *my* chocolates. And I find *this* in the basket." Sebastian fished in his pocket and pulled something out and threw it on the ground at Jonathan's feet.

It was a little paper crane. Carefully folded. And all crumpled up.

"And I come back down here and, *surprise*, Johnny's gone! And what do we find under his pillow?" Sebastian rummaged through his other pocket and threw something else to the floor. Without looking, Jonathan knew it was his parents' letter, folded neatly into a perfect bird.

"So, Johnny, you tell me . . . how stupid do you think I am?"

Jonathan looked back and forth between the two paper cranes, then back up at Sebastian.

"I don't think you're stupid. I think you're mad. And I think you're right. Colin took your chocolates. I *know* you're right. But I don't know where he is. That's the truth."

"You already told me that if you *did* know, you wouldn't tell me."

Jonathan nodded and pinched his top lip between his teeth. He looked away, out the window at the storm clouds piled atop one another above Slabhenge's crumbling walls.

"Yeah. And I wouldn't." Then he looked at Sebastian. "I *won't*. But I haven't seen him. I promise."

Sebastian licked the angry spittle from his lips. He blinked and blew out a breath and looked away. He opened his mouth to say something, but Benny butted in first.

"You can't trust him, Sebastian."

Jonathan's hands balled into anxious fists. He didn't like the eager edge to Benny's voice. The way his eyes were shining and his mouth opened and closed. Like a snake coiled and about to strike.

"Shut up, Benny, I—" Sebastian started to say.

"You can't trust him," Benny said again. "I know why he's here."

Sebastian's head turned slowly to look at Benny. His eyebrows scrunched together.

"What do you mean?"

"Don't," Jonathan said quietly, his eyes locked on Benny's.

"I peeked at his papers. In the Admiral's office, when he first got here," Benny said. His eyes stayed with Jonathan. The corners of his pudgy mouth teased toward a smile. "You can't trust him, Sebastian. Do you know what he did?"

"Don't," Jonathan pleaded again. He rubbed at his arms with his hands.

"What?" Sebastian asked. The whole room hung in waiting silence. Only the windows shook and spoke, straining to hold back the storm that fought to rush inside.

"I know why he doesn't like fire," Benny said, his smile ripening into a sickening sneer.

Jonathan shook his head.

"Little Johnny here," Benny said, savoring every bloody word like a vampire, "is a *murderer.*"

Jonathan's jaw clenched down to steel.

"No," he said through his teeth.

"Oh, yes. A murderer. And do you know who he killed?"

Jonathan tried to stand up, but hard hands on his shoulders held him down.

"You shut up," he said, his voice cracking. Already, Benny was blurred, standing before him.

"He murdered his little sister. Sophia. Set a fire and burned their house down, with her trapped inside."

"Shut up!" Jonathan screamed, fighting at the hands that held him down.

"It's true!" Benny shouted back, stepping toward him. "Show them your arms!"

"No!" Jonathan howled. "Don't!"

"Pull back his sleeves! Look at his arms!" Benny crowed.

Jonathan, totally blinded now by his tears, felt his sleeves yanked back to his elbows. The room gasped, then hushed. The hands let him go. He closed his eyes, his body racked by sobs.

"God," Sebastian said. His voice was hollow, shocked.

"No," Jonathan tried to say, but he wasn't sure his voice made it through his choked throat.

He rubbed at his sightless eyes with his arms, forgetting that his sleeves were pulled up. The scarred and hardened tissue of his burns and scars scraped roughly on his face.

"Leave me alone," he managed to gasp, his voice echoing in the still chamber. "You don't know how much I loved her. How much I *love* her." But he couldn't tell anymore what he was saying from what he was merely feeling. It could have been that the words he meant to say only echoed, unheard, in the dank dungeon of his harrowed heart.

"I saw," Benny said, his voice low and stained with a stinking smile. "I saw the psychiatrist's report about your therapy. About your guilt over the burning death of your sister. I saw the doctor's report about your burns. And I saw your sentencing papers. For arson."

Jonathan just shook his head and kept his eyes closed.

"God," Sebastian said again, his voice dripping with disgust. "You're a freak. No wonder you want to stay here."

The windows shivered in their panes. The cold and endless dripping of water filled the edges of the silence.

"You better tell us," Sebastian said. "I want him back. He's a rat."

"I don't know where he is," Jonathan sniffed.

"Fine. Whatever. But you'll find out. He'll try to talk to you. And then you'll hand him over."

Sebastian turned and walked back toward the stairs that led to his room. His feet sloshed slowly from one puddle to the next. The tip of the sword dragged with a jagged scrape along the stone floor. He stopped at the bottom stair.

"You have until tomorrow night. If you don't give him to us by then, you have to go after him. And you can't come back without him. You can starve out there with him and the other rats." Sebastian coughed out a nasty little laugh. "The freak and the rat. Best friends in the nuthouse."

176

His steps receded up the staircase.

Everyone else stood in damp quiet.

Then, one by one, they turned and walked away. Walter was the last to go. He took a small step toward Jonathan, his eyes wide, and then stopped. He opened his mouth like he was going to say something. But then he shook his head and turned away, leaving Jonathan sitting alone in the hard chair, tears running unwiped down his face like the rain on the dark windows, his horrible scars exposed.

CHAPTER TWENTY-ONE
FIRES AND FLOWERS

Jonathan didn't take the turn that would bring him down past the Hatch and up to the library. He walked right by it, moving slow to protect his candle's fragile flame. He didn't have any matches. There hadn't been a chance to grab a lantern. The thin white candle was the only light he had.

He pressed forward through the darkness, stopping from time to time to listen. All he ever heard, besides his breathing and the ever-present dripping, was the papery scrape of tiny claws on wet stone.

"Colin?" he whisper-shouted. His voice came back to him in damp echoes. There was no answer.

He climbed a short staircase, then descended a longer, spiral one. He passed a narrow window set high in the wall. There was no glass—just a narrow, tombstone-shaped opening in the wall, a couple of feet tall. The wind blew spatters of icy rain into the passageway. Jonathan had to stand on the tips of his toes to peer out at the ocean that surrounded them. Dark clouds were stacked and heaped to the horizon, just as they had been since he arrived. They looked grimmer now, though, more threatening. Like they were coming for him. The waves jostled and crowded one another like an angry mob storming Slabhenge Castle.

He kept going, leaving the gray light of the window

behind, returning to the world of claw scrapes and candlelight.

"Colin?"

He turned a sharp corner into a hallway that was narrower, tight. He passed one door, closed and silent. Then another. Then one that hung open, the door dangling from a single broken hinge; the room behind it was small and dark and empty. Inside was only a broken chair and some empty bottles littered on the floor.

The fourth door was closed and Jonathan was just past it when something caught his eye. Something small and white on the floor, barely within the reach of his candle's wavering light. He stopped and bent down.

It was a paper crane. Tiny. Not much bigger than a marble.

Jonathan smiled and stood up. He pushed the door open with an echoing creak.

Beyond was a steep, skinny staircase that circled up into shadows. Jonathan walked up it, letting the door swing closed behind him.

It was a long staircase, rising in a tight spiral. Up and up and up until Jonathan knew that he wasn't just climbing a staircase; he was climbing one of Slabhenge's towers.

At the top was another door, open just an inch. He pressed his hand against the knotty wood and pushed the door open.

The room was perfectly round, with a high, coned ceiling. In the middle was a thin mattress covered in a rumpled pile of blankets. On the far side of the room, Colin sat in a straight-backed chair, looking out a round window.

He turned and gave Jonathan one of his short-lived smiles.

"You found my little bird," he said.

"Yeah." Jonathan stepped into the room. It had four circular windows, one looking in each direction. The glass was broken out of one of them. There was a puddle of rainwater on the floor beneath it. A chilled wet breeze spun through the room.

Colin shivered.

"There'th a thtorm coming."

"Probably."

"Definitely."

Jonathan crossed over to one of the windows. It looked inward to Slabhenge, down onto the courtyard. He could see Tony and Miguel halfheartedly kicking the ball back and forth. They looked small and far away. They looked like little kids.

"Do you want a chocolate?" Colin asked.

Jonathan looked at him and smiled. Colin smiled back.

"No, thanks. He'll probably check my breath when I get back."

Colin's smile widened.

"He'th pretty mad, huh?"

Jonathan's smile dropped away.

"More than pretty mad, Colin. You need to be careful. You shouldn't sneak down anymore. I—don't know what he'll do to you."

Colin shrugged.

"I'm careful. Everyone is athleep when I come down. Or eating. And I know all the wayth to ethcape now."

"What do you mean?"

Colin's eyes widened and an excited smile spread across his face.

"Thith plathe ith really amathing. All the hallth and stairth and roomth are connected. There are almotht no dead endth. It'th like an anthill. All turnth and loopth and thircleth. And I know it. Or motht of it. He'd never catch me."

Jonathan shook his head.

"Don't risk it, Colin. You can't let him catch you. He's kind of . . . losing it, I think. And I can't . . ." Jonathan's voice broke off. He frowned and bit his lip. "I can't protect you anymore. He won't listen to me now."

Colin tilted his head and blinked.

"What happened?" he asked. Jonathan looked away, out the window, then back to Colin.

"They think I know where you are. Well, they thought I knew where you were. And Benny . . . Benny told them some stuff."

"What? What did he thay?"

Jonathan swallowed and took a deep breath.

"He said that he'd looked through my paperwork. He showed them my—my scars." Jonathan rubbed at his arms. "He told them I was sent here for . . . for . . . murdering my little sister. Sophia." Jonathan's voice caught when he said the name. His breaths were fast and shallow and they burned in his throat. His voice scratched down into a whisper. "He told them I started a fire. And that she died. He told them I killed my little sister." Tears, as hot as the rain was cold, dropped from his eyes and down his cheeks.

Colin frowned. His eyes squinted into Jonathan's face.

"It ithn't true, though," he said.

Jonathan's throat tightened like a punch-ready fist. His eyes burned like deadly fire. He ripped a ragged breath from his lungs and looked away.

"Oh," Colin said, his voice a breathless whisper. "It *ith* true."

Jonathan rubbed at his tears with his wrist. He looked away, through his tears, out the window at the storm.

"Tell me, Jonathan," Colin said softly. "Tell me what happened."

Jonathan wiped at his face with a sleeve. "It doesn't matter."

Colin stood up and walked over to where Jonathan stood.

"It doth. It *doth* matter. Tell me."

Jonathan took a shuddering lungful of air. His teeth chattered when he exhaled.

"I . . . I . . . used to start fires. I don't know why. I don't even remember how it started. I liked to . . . watch the flames. Watch them grow. See something that I'd built get hot and bright and alive. I don't know." He looked up, for just a second, into Colin's eyes, then away again quickly.

"Little ones at first, then bigger. Then I set one at school. In the bathroom. But I got caught running away. I got in big trouble. Parents called in, kicked out of school, the whole thing. It was awful. I didn't start a fire for a while. And then . . . and then . . ." He stopped, the words stuck in his throat like ash. His teeth clenched hard and with one deep breath through his nose, he plunged forward.

"And then I started again. Small ones. In wastebaskets. At night, when everyone was sleeping. Sophia caught me. She was so mad. She was afraid I was gonna get in trouble again. She made me promise not to do it ever again. She . . . she even took the matches I had." Jonathan's voice got smaller and smaller as he spoke. He wanted to walk away, to slam the door, to retreat to the shadows with his raging. But Colin still stood there with his listening eyes before the storm-darkened window, and Jonathan's words stumbled on.

"And then. That night. It was . . . like a nightmare. The smoke. The flames climbing up the walls. So much smoke. I wanted to run. And then I heard her. Downstairs. Screaming my name. And the fire was just so hot. Growing so fast." He looked up through burning, blurry eyes. "It was like a monster, Colin. It was *roaring*." His voice was cut off by a choking sob. "I could hear her. But I couldn't save her. And she died in the fire. Screaming for me to save her."

Colin swallowed, his own eyes full, his fingers tugging at the skin of his neck.

"That'th why. Why you were on the Thinner'th Thorrow. You think it'th your fault."

"It *is* my fault!" Jonathan shouted, his voice hoarse and raw. "I killed my sister! I let her die!"

Colin took a step closer.

"Jonathan," he said. "It wath an acthident. Jutht a terrible acthident."

Jonathan shook his head angrily and wiped the tears out of his eyes with his wrist.

"My parents say the same thing. That it was an accident. That it wasn't my fault. How much they love me." He looked up into Colin's eyes. "But I can still hear her screaming, Colin. Screaming for *me*. It shouldn't be me at home with them. It should be Sophia." He took a shaky, broken breath. "I'm probably the only one of all of us that actually deserves to be here."

There was a moment of nothing but wind and the smell of rain and, somewhere out on the darkness of the sea, a low rumble of thunder.

Then Colin's thoughtful eyes narrowed.

"But . . . how did you get the thcars?" he asked.

Jonathan sniffed and cleared his throat and took a step away.

"I better go. Sebastian'll be getting suspicious. And you need to stay out of the way, Colin. Don't let him catch you."

Colin squinted and bit his lip. He seemed about to say something, then stopped. He nodded, once. Then he asked, "Are you going to be okay?"

"I'll be fine."

Jonathan opened the door and put his foot on the top step.

"Don't you think they mith you?"

Jonathan stopped. He didn't have to ask who Colin was talking about.

"You're the only one who geth a letter every thingle day. Don't you think they mith you? Don't you think lothing *one* of their children wath enough?"

Jonathan's eyebrows frowned. He chewed on his lip.

"Don't you mith them? Don't you mith home?"

Jonathan didn't turn around. When he answered, his voice echoed down the winding staircase.

"I do," he said, incredibly softly. Like a secret he was keeping from himself. "I do." He focused his eyes on the flame clutched in his hand.

"I went every day to Sophia's grave and put a flower on it. Every single day. She loved flowers. My parents promised that they'd do it for me while I was gone."

He closed his eyes, then opened them and looked back at Colin. His eyes took in the stone floor, the stone walls, the puddle and the shadows.

"There's no flowers here."

When the door closed on the round room, Colin was still standing pinching his neck, a thoughtful frown on his face.

When Jonathan returned to the dining room, they were just starting their nightly letter home. No one spoke to him. The dining room was again awash in candlelight and the whispers of pens on paper. Jonathan's letter was short. But he was the last one done. Benny read it and rolled his eyes and said, "Fine. Night-night, Johnny." Jonathan didn't reply, or even look Benny in the face. He supposed that he should have glared at him. Stared him down. He supposed that he should hate Benny. But Jonathan didn't have any hate left. He'd already used it all on himself.

When Jonathan went to his mattress to go to sleep, he found that the ring of seven mattresses had shrunk to three. Most of the other boys had dragged theirs away into a different corner. Away from him. Only Walter and David had stayed.

The two boys looked at him from around the slowly dancing candle flame between them.

Jonathan put his head down and closed his eyes.

"Aren't you gonna read, man?" Walter asked.

"You still want me to?"

"Yeah. Don't you have another book?"

"Um-hmm." Jonathan rolled over and fished *Treasure Island* out from where he'd stowed it under his pillow. He looked up at the faces of Walter and David, waiting in the yellow glow of the candles.

"You sure?" he asked. They both nodded.

He cleared his throat.

"*Chapter One*," he began, his voice still a wounded whisper. It gained strength as he read. "*The Old Sea Dog at the Admiral Benbow.*"

In the morning, when he awoke, there was a new piece of paper lying on the pillow beside his head. It was not a crane.

The paper on his pillow was folded into the shape of a perfect flower. The flower had a shiny gold center.

A dark brown square of chocolate sat beside it.

Dear Mom and Dad,

I miss you. Thank you for the letters.

I'm sorry. Not for what you think. For everything else. I really am.

Please give my love to Sophia.

Love,
Jonathan

CHAPTER TWENTY-TWO
CAUGHT

"Last chance, Johnny boy." Sebastian's voice was a snarl. Outside, the wind howled with fierce strength between the crumbling towers of Slabhenge. Lightning flashed on puddles growing and spreading across the courtyard stones. Thunder scared the window glass into shaking.

The storm had been growing all day. Jonathan had watched it rage and strengthen through the windows. He'd been locked inside during the mail exchange. He hadn't bothered going to see the librarian or Colin. He knew he'd have plenty of time for that when Sebastian banished him. It had been a long day. He'd read most of *Treasure Island*.

But now the sun had set. The day was over. His deadline had expired. All the world was dropping into storm and darkness.

"I don't know where he is," Jonathan lied.

"Liar."

Jonathan looked away. He was seated at one of the long dining room tables. Benny and Francis stood on either side of him. All the other boys were standing around, watching nervously.

"Fine. It's your funeral." Sebastian pushed a paper and pen across the table to him. "Write what I say. *Exactly* what I say. Benny, check his work."

Jonathan pursed his lips, then picked up the pen. There was no use fighting. It would only make things worse.

"Dear Mom and Dad," Sebastian started, and Jonathan rolled his eyes and copied the words onto the paper. "Everything is going fine. The food is good and I'm learning a lot." Sebastian lowered his voice. "Add an exclamation point to that. Make it look cheerful." His eyes rose to the ceiling in concentration. "I won't be able to write for a while. We are . . ." Sebastian paused and squinted one eye, drumming his lips with his fingers. "We are getting ready for a big test. I love you and miss you lots. Love, Johnny."

"You really want me to sign it 'Johnny'?"

Sebastian lowered his eyes and glared across the table.

"Love, Jonathan."

Jonathan's pen scratched across the paper and then he set it down.

"How'd he do, Benny?"

"Fine. He wrote just what you said."

Sebastian rose to his feet.

"That's your last letter home, Johnny." He looked past Jonathan to the kids standing behind him. "Give him a couple candles. And a book of matches." His eyes dropped back down to Jonathan and he smiled. "Although I don't know if we can really trust him with matches."

With an echoing crash, the door to the courtyard swung open and smashed into the stone wall. They all jumped and turned. Rain blew through the open door, splattering the dark stone wall. Some of the candles they'd lit blew out in the wind that blustered in among them.

"Damn it, close that door, Reggie!" Sebastian shouted. Lightning flashed, and a rumble of thunder cracked, sounding unnaturally loud through the open door. "And make sure it's closed *all the way* this time!"

When the storm was once again locked mostly outside, Sebastian turned back to Jonathan.

"Say hi to the little rat for me. I hope you two have lots of fun."

Jonathan was jerked to his feet. Candles and matches were pressed into his hand. Sebastian stalked around the table and poked him with the sword.

"Go on," he said, prodding Jonathan toward the door that led into Slabhenge's dark interior. "Go ahead and find your friend. And don't come crawling back here. You two made your choice."

He was pushed through the doorway, into the familiar musty shadows of the corridor.

"Good night," Sebastian's voice echoed after him. "Sleep tight."

With trembling fingers, Jonathan struck a match. He held the sputtering flame to a candle wick, then quickly dropped it with a hiss into a puddle at his feet. The rain was falling even harder now than it had been the morning the Admiral and his men were struck down. Slabhenge, inside and out, was all dripping and puddles.

Jonathan bit his teeth together hard and started off into the darkness.

It took him a while to find Colin's tower hideout. He'd been wandering the first time he'd found it and this time he had to circle and peer and look for landmarks. He remembered what Colin had said about everything in Slabhenge being connected, and kept walking. He stopped from time to time to listen; the rats seemed more than normally large and active, especially behind him. Maybe it was the storm, which was howling and thundering loud enough to be heard even through the thick stone walls.

At one point as he wandered he passed one of the staircases that he knew led down to the Hatch. It was wild tonight, knocking and rocking and echoing up from the darkness. Like a demon thrashing against chains ready to break. He swallowed and pressed on, looking for Colin's refuge.

And then, there it was. The long hallway with the four doors, the little paper bird hiding in the darkness. Jonathan slipped through the door and up the stairs.

Colin was sitting on his bed. Paper, some folded and some not, lay scattered and piled on the bed and floor around him. Four candles sat around the bed on the floor. Startling splashes of white light flashed through the windows from the storm outside. Colin was facing the door, chewing on a bright red apple.

"Hey," he said with a smile as brief and bright as the lightning. "I wath hoping that wath you."

A ferocious blast of wind whistled in through the broken window, shuffling the loose leaves of paper into a swirl of scattered white. One of the candles flickered out. When the gust had died down, Colin calmly relit the smoking wick with one of the other candles.

"You're here late," Colin said.

Jonathan took a couple of steps into the room.

"I'm here for good."

"What do you mean?"

"Sebastian. He said I had to leave. I'm, like, kicked out."

Colin's brow furrowed and he pinched at his neck with one hand.

"I thought he wanted to catch me."

"Yeah. He does."

Colin squinted one eye and cocked his head.

"Well . . . don't you think he'd jutht follow you?"

Jonathan opened his mouth. But before he could say anything, he heard the distant creak of a door from behind him, and then the rumble of footsteps running up the stairs.

The lightning was constant and explosive and spectacular. It provided more light to the dining room than the candles that were lit on every table. Colin sat in a chair in the middle of the room, flanked by Roger and Francis.

Rain pelted the huge windows. Thunder booms like cannon shots rattled the glass. The courtyard was a rain-lashed lake, reflecting the violent white cracks of lightning above. The wind shrieked between Slabhenge's tall towers like an army of furious ghosts.

The sword glowed red and yellow in Sebastian's hand, from the candlelight. Except when it gleamed white in the lightning. The Admiral's hat was back on his head, retrieved from Colin's room. His sneering mouth was busy chewing one of the reclaimed gold-wrapped chocolates.

Jonathan stood off to one side with the others. Benny was holding him roughly with one hand, pinching harder than he needed to, his fingers like fangs in Jonathan's shoulder. Jonathan sniffed from time to time and rubbed at his nose with his arm. His sleeve was smeared with dark blood. When the boys had reached the top of the stairs to Colin's room, he'd tried quickly to slam the door, but it was too late; they'd burst in and Sebastian had knocked him to the ground with one vicious punch. Colin was bleeding, too, from a cut above his eye that Sebastian had given him when he'd tried to dash to the broken window and toss the Admiral's hat out.

"Admit it, Colin, you're the one who stole my chocolates."

"Of courth I am. You found them in my room, Thebathtian."

"Shut up. So you admit it, then, trespassing and theft."

"Yeth. I went into the Admiral'th room and took the Admiral'th chocolateth."

"*It's my room!*" Sebastian shouted, getting right in Colin's face. "*The Admiral is dead! I'm in charge! When are you going to get that?*"

"Oh, I get it, Thebathtian." Colin's voice was calm. Soft. Sad. "I abtholutely get it."

Sebastian straightened back up. His face was eerily pale in the shifting light.

"And we all saw what you did to the Sinner's Sorrow. That's destruction of property. You have to be punished."

There was an especially loud crack of thunder at the same moment as a particularly forceful gale of wind. One of the large windows shattered, sending shards of glass flying into the group of boys. They screamed and ducked and dove under tables. Rain blew in through the broken window. Wind whipped through the room, blowing out most of the candles.

"Hold that little thief!" Sebastian hollered. "Relight those candles!" The boys stood frozen, their eyes wide and scared. "Oh, Jesus, guys, it's just a little thunderstorm. Relight those candles. We'll cover the window in the morning."

They got the candles relit and moved to tables farther from the broken window. They all shivered wetly in the storm that was now in the room with them.

"Punishment," Sebastian continued. His black hair was plastered to his forehead with rain. Water dripped down his face. He had to almost shout to be heard above the wind and the thunder and the pouring rain. "The Sinner's Sorrow is ruined. So what could we do? What could we do to a thief and a criminal?"

The group blinked at him in silence. Teeth chattered.

"In some places, they cut a thief's hand off," Sebastian said. He held the sword up and looked at it, turning the blade to catch the light. His mouth widened into a grim smile. The tips of his teeth showed whitely. The group tensed. "But that would be too messy." He stepped slowly closer to Colin and his captors. "In other places, they just mark a thief. They carve a *T* into his forehead. Or his arm. Or his chest." The smile disappeared. "Put him on the table," he said. "Hold him down."

"No!" Jonathan cried, and Benny's arm jerked around his neck, holding him in a headlock.

Colin wiggled and fought, but he was too small. The older boys wrestled him onto a table on his back and pinned him down.

The lightning flashed. Thunder cracked so loudly the boys could feel it in their chests. It sounded like the thunder was coming from inside the prison.

"Come on, Sebastian! This is messed up!" Tony argued.

"Shut up!" Sebastian's voice was wild and furious. His face was twisted in anger. It was all white and black in the flashing light. It looked like a mask. "Open him up! Bare his chest!" he commanded, and the goons obeyed. Buttons popped and Colin's skin shone white in the twisted light. Sebastian stepped forward, brandishing the sword.

Jonathan twisted with a surge of energy and broke loose from Benny's hold. He ran toward Sebastian.

Sebastian turned to face him just as Jonathan slipped in a puddle on the floor. He hit the stone floor with a hard splash. He pulled himself quickly up to his hands and knees, but then Sebastian's booted foot swung into his side like a sledgehammer. All the breath was kicked out of his lungs with a piercing whoosh of pain and he rolled over onto his back.

Sebastian stepped forward and pressed a foot onto Jonathan's neck. It was wet and cold and hard. Jonathan blinked and gasped for breath. His feet kicked in the puddle. His hands tugged at Sebastian's leg, but Sebastian just pressed down harder.

The sword blade swung slowly around until it was inches from Jonathan's face, sharp and silver and dripping rain onto his nose.

"You're next, Johnny," Sebastian said.

Behind them, the door crashed open, letting in another mighty gust of wind.

"Damn it, Reggie, I told you—" Sebastian started, before he turned and looked and stopped.

They all did.

Someone was standing in the doorway.

A stranger. On Slabhenge. Looking at them all standing there in the storm-drenched dining room.

"I came to warn ye about the storm!" he shouted. It was Patrick, the guy from the boat. He was wearing a yellow rain slicker and he was out of breath.

The boys all stood, frozen, in the lightning and the flickering candlelight.

Patrick's eyes seemed to focus. He saw Colin, bloody and pinned down on top of the table. He saw the Sinner's Sorrow standing in splinters. He saw Sebastian, soaked and furious and wearing the Admiral's hat. He saw Jonathan, lying on the floor with a bloody nose and a boot on his throat and sword to his face.

"Where is everybody? What in the world is going on here?" he asked, taking a step back.

Sebastian raised his sword and pointed it at Patrick.

"Grab him," he said.

CHAPTER TWENTY-FOUR
ALL THE GROWN-UPS ARE DEAD AND GONE

After a few minutes, Patrick sat straining and panting, tied firmly to a chair. He'd been too surprised at first to run when the pack of wild boys had rushed him. They'd caught and tangled him in a tidal wave of arms and hands and pulled him to the ground.

Then he'd started fighting. At first, he'd gained ground. He'd wrestled and twisted and was almost free when he'd felt the tip of Sebastian's sword pressed against his neck. "Don't move an inch," Sebastian had warned. "Not an inch."

Patrick had frozen, an arm around his neck, others pinning his arms to his sides, his lungs heaving, and looked into Sebastian's eyes. He must not have seen any bluff there. He was tied up and walked to the chair where he sat, looking around with wide eyes at the savage boys.

Sebastian was pacing. He was grinding his teeth and idly swinging his sword. His eyes darted around the dark room. His shadow, thrown onto the wet stone walls by white flashes of lightning, loomed and jumped as he walked.

"Where is everybody?" Patrick asked again.

"We're all right here," Sebastian said with a sneer, holding his arms open.

"Yeah, but—what about the Admiral? Mr. Vander? Where are all the grown-ups?"

Benny, who was standing guard by Patrick's side, leaned in close to his face with a toothy sneer.

"All the grown-ups are dead and gone," he said. "And that's just how we like it."

Patrick looked at him like he was crazy.

"What d'ye mean? Ye mean . . . ye killed 'em?"

"No!" Sebastian shouted, spinning in a puddle. "We had nothing to do with it! It was lightning. They were all struck by lightning!"

Patrick gulped and looked around at the ring of frightened faces.

"What . . . *all* of them?"

"Yes, *all* of them!" Sebastian yelled, stamping his foot in the puddle. "We had nothing to do with it!"

Patrick licked his lips and shrugged.

"Okay. This *is* a crazy storm," he added, nodding with his chin at the raging tempest howling through the broken window.

"No, no," Sebastian said, resuming his pacing. "Not tonight. The last storm. What . . . five days ago?"

Patrick went pale. His eyes widened even farther.

"Five days? Ye've all been here by yerselves fer five days?"

Sebastian stopped his walking and glared at him.

"Yes. And we've been fine. Just fine."

Patrick's eyes darted to the shattered Sinner's Sorrow, to Colin's bloody head and Jonathan's bloody nose.

"Aye," he said carefully. "Sure ye have."

"But now we've got a new problem," Sebastian continued. "What to do with you?"

"I think ye should let me go," Patrick tried.

"No," Sebastian said with a small smile. "Then our game is over. And I'm not ready for that. I don't want to go back just yet. None of us do."

"I do."

"Shut up, Colin. Of course *you* do. We'll get to you in a second. First . . . what do we do with *him*?"

All eyes turned to Patrick. He looked nervously around.

"We could put him in the freezer with the grown-ups," someone suggested.

"Nah," Sebastian said. "That wouldn't be very nice. Anywhere out of the way will be fine. How about the coal room, for now?" He nodded to Roger and Gregory. "Take him down there. Leave a lantern on for him."

"Wait!" Patrick protested. "Ye never listened to why I came! There's a monstrous storm coming on. It be a hundred-year storm, they say. A hurricane. Class Five! Bringing a terrible storm surge with it, too, historic high tides. Why, it could wash this whole place away! They told me I was mad to even try and make it out here, but I couldn't leave ye all to drown."

Sebastian rolled his eyes.

"Take him away," he repeated.

"Ye've got to listen to me!"

"We're in a stone castle," Sebastian replied, his voice bored. "Built on a stone island. It's been here for hundreds of years. Islands don't sink."

"Yes, they do."

Everyone turned to Jonathan.

"It's true. This place is crumbling. The island is getting smaller. There used to be a beach and everything." He looked around at the silent faces. "It's true! Think of those stairs leading down into the water from the gate. The whole bottom floor is already under water—that's what the Hatch is!"

Sebastian blew his breath out through flapping lips.

"Uh-huh. Nice try. Shut up, Jonathan." He looked back to the kids standing around Patrick. "Take him away. Now."

The boys stumbled away, dragging Patrick roughly between them. Sebastian paced back and forth while they were gone, his feet splashing in storm-water puddles.

"Listen, man," Miguel said. "You gotta calm down and—"

"Shut up," Sebastian snarled with wild eyes. He shook the sword in his hand. "We're gonna be fine. All of us. As long as you keep your mouth shut, you'll be fine, too."

When the boys returned from the coal room, Sebastian turned and cocked an eyebrow at Colin.

"Now. Back to *you*. And your punishment."

Colin frantically shook his head. Gerald and Francis were holding him tight on top of the table, but now he was sitting up.

"Pleath don't cut me, Thebathtian."

Sebastian rolled his eyes again.

"I was never gonna cut you," he snorted. Colin's eyes narrowed doubtfully. "I *wasn't*. Jesus. I was just trying to scare you." Colin's body visibly relaxed. Until Sebastian continued talking. "Besides, I have something *better* planned for you."

The wind was an unending high howl now, as if the whole of the tortured sky was one great furious beast. It screamed through the broken window, bringing rain and chilling salty spray with it. The lightning was so constant that the moments of darkness between were more eerie and surprising than the flashes themselves.

"You two, bring him," Sebastian said to Roger and Gregory, lifting his chin toward Jonathan. They grabbed him roughly by his elbows. "And you guys bring him," he added to Francis and Gerald, still holding down Colin. He whispered something into Benny's ear, who nodded and ran off to the kitchen.

Sebastian stalked off toward the darkened doorway that led into the interior of Slabhenge. He paused at the exit. He gripped the sword in his teeth while he used both hands to light a candle, then looked at the crowd of boys waiting at the tables.

"All of you, follow me. Bring a candle." He smiled, a dangerous smile full of sharp, white teeth that glistened in the lightning. "It's time to find out what Colin's punishment is."

CHAPTER TWENTY-FIVE
A CRASH AND A BANG

They all followed Sebastian through the dark, winding tunnels of Slabhenge's twisting corridors and staircases. It wasn't clear where they were going, or even if Sebastian had a destination in mind. But whenever Sebastian came to a choice between two halls, he chose the darker and narrower one. Whenever he had to choose between staircases, he chose down.

In a winding, candlelit line they passed through the dip that went by the Hatch. It was only feet away, down that last cramped stairway and around a corner. It was a riot of violent, eerie noises, louder than Jonathan had ever heard it. Bangs and shudders and thirsty slurps and the high, pained squeaking of straining iron. Some boys slowed down on the landing that led down to the Hatch. Most shivered and sped up.

Finally, they came to a dark little windowless room, small and wet and cold at the bottom of a crumbling staircase. It was an especially desolate and forgotten corner of the madhouse island. Rats hurried out as the boys came in with their splashing feet and flickering flames, brushing past their feet, causing some boys to cry out and jump.

All together, the group nearly filled the room. The ceiling was low and dripping green slime. Even here, though, they could hear the storm raging away beyond the thick stone walls that surrounded them. It sounded far, and angry, and above them, like they were belowground.

"Here we are," Sebastian said with satisfaction. "It's perfect."

The last kids in were Benny and James. Benny had a rope over his shoulder and a sack in his hands. James was carrying a wooden chair. Sebastian took the chair and set it in the middle of the little floor. Its legs wobbled on the uneven stone. Colin was thunked down in the chair and tied firmly to it with the rope.

"Make sure it's good and tight," Sebastian said. When the knots were all tightened and Sebastian had checked them, he stood back and looked at Colin.

"You wanted to sneak around and steal like a little rat. Fine. Benny came up with the perfect punishment. You get to spend the night with the rats. All by yourself." Colin was panting, his forehead beaded with sweat. He pulled against the ropes binding him, but there was no give. "The bag, please, Benny," Sebastian said, holding out his hand. He reached inside and pulled out a handful of something. "We want to make sure the rats know their new roommate is here," he said, holding his hand up to the light. It was full of crackers and bits of cheese from the kitchen. Looking Colin in the eye, he scattered the food around Colin on the floor. He reached into the sack for another handful and tossed it on the floor leading to the stairs. Pulling out one more handful, he crumbled it together in his hand and sprinkled it onto Colin's lap.

The boys all stood in silence, watching wide-eyed.

"That should do it," Sebastian said, rubbing his hands on his pant legs. "You should have *lots* of little friends tonight. Come on, let's go."

"You're jutht gonna leave me here?"

"You got it. Not forever. One long night oughta be enough to teach you a lesson, I think. We can talk more in the morning, you and I."

The rest of the boys were already starting to plod back up the stairs. No one said a word. As each kid left with his candle, the room got darker and darker.

The last ones left were Sebastian, Benny, Jonathan, and the two goons holding him.

"Aren't you going to leave me a light, at leatht?"

"Oh. Sure, Colin. Here you go." Sebastian took a candle from one of the kids leaving and held it out toward Colin. His fingers opened, and the candle fell to the floor. It sputtered and hissed and went out in a puddle. "Oops. Sorry about that. Good night, Colin."

"Sebastian, seriously, you can't . . ." Jonathan began.

Sebastian's head swung like a hunting panther to Jonathan.

"I can, Johnny," he seethed. "I can. You had your chance. You picked your side. You'll get yours after dinner. Don't worry."

Jonathan struggled against the boys holding him, but it was no use. He was dragged up the stairs behind Sebastian and Benny and the last candle. The last he saw of Colin, he was sitting in the growing blackness, eyes wide and lips trembling, all alone.

Jonathan tried to pay attention as they made their way back to the dining room. At one point he thought they were close to where the library was, but they never saw it. The Hatch, when they passed it, was making an unholy racket. Like an army of watery demons on the other side, raging to get in. No boys paused to listen this time.

They all stopped cold when they got back to the dining room. There were no longer puddles in the room—the entire floor was under an inch of water. It was black and dappled by rain blowing in through the window. The light of the candles still burning on the tables was reflected eerily on its surface.

Lightning crackled, filling the windows with blinding light. There was a great boom of thunder that made them all jump.

"No letter writing tonight," Sebastian said, looking at the flooded room. "We can do it first thing in the morning, after the storm. Dinnertime."

"Uh, Sebastian, this isn't okay," David said cautiously.

"It's fine. A little water won't hurt us. It's just 'cause the window's broken."

"Where are we gonna sleep, man?" Walter asked, pointing at their waterlogged mattresses still lying on the floor.

"You can bring your beds upstairs for tonight. There's plenty of room."

"Sebastian," Jonathan said. "Remember what Patrick said about the storm and the surge and—"

"Shut up, Jonathan. No one cares what Patrick said. Don't piss me off—I'm still deciding what your punishment is." He looked at Gregory and Roger. "One of you keep your hands on him at all times. I know the little punk'll run away to save his little friend first chance he gets."

They ate dinner sitting on the tables, their feet on the chairs. The storm was so loud they couldn't talk over it. They kept having to relight their candles, blown out by the hard fists of gusting wind that hammered through the room. Jonathan sat where Sebastian had been carving with his sword a couple of days ago, flanked by a guard on either side. He fingered the crudely notched letters Sebastian had inscribed on the wooden tabletop: S-C-A-R-S. He looked around at the soggy boys glumly eating, shivering and soaked, sitting in near-darkness with rain blowing in the broken window. His mind kept circling around Colin, bound in blackness, swarmed by giant rats. He couldn't swallow a bite.

"We need to keep the furnace lit!" Sebastian shouted over the storm. "Jonathan—it's your turn! You two go with him!" He tossed a stale roll to Roger. "You can give that to our prisoner. Don't untie him, though!"

Jonathan managed to eat a dry bite of bread and slumped down to the coal room, Roger and Gregory right behind.

Patrick was tied to his chair in the middle of the room under a dangling lantern, surrounded by piles of coal. The furnace glowed and hissed behind him. His face was grim and he was drenched in sweat. Jonathan gasped and unbuttoned the top button of his own shirt. He'd forgotten how hot it was in the dark little cellar. There was a large puddle at the foot of the stairs. Jonathan frowned. He didn't remember the coal room having any puddles.

"Have ye come to yer senses, then?" Patrick asked.

"We're just here to feed the furnace," Roger said. "Here." He held out the roll.

Patrick looked at it, his hands tied behind his back.

"Uh, ye'll have to untie me."

"No way," Roger answered. He tore a chunk off the roll and shoved it into Patrick's mouth. "Get to work, Jonathan," he said over his shoulder. "I don't wanna be down here forever."

Jonathan was looking at the puddle on the ground. It was spreading and growing as he watched. He looked closer and saw the little rivulets of water running down the stairs along the wall.

"Water's getting down here," he said, pointing. "From upstairs."

"Who cares?"

"Well, that means—"

"Look, just get to work, okay? I'll help."

Jonathan and Gregory started shoveling coal into the wheelbarrow while Roger fed Patrick bites of roll.

"Ye boys are crazy," Patrick said when they stood gasping for breath after dumping the first load into the fiery furnace. "Ye can't keep going like this. Ye need to get outta here."

"Quiet," Roger said. "We're fine."

"What happened to yer nose?" he asked, looking at Jonathan. Jonathan sniffed and touched it gingerly with sooty fingers. It was still sore.

"Nothing. Just an accident."

"Aye," Patrick said quietly. "I bet plenty of accidents happen around that boy with the sword."

"Come on. Keep shoveling. I wanna go to bed."

They were just about to open the furnace doors for the second load of coal when they heard the crash from above them.

More than a crash. A shattering, shuddering explosion that echoed down the stairs. They froze in mid-motion, then turned to look at the staircase.

There was a moment of near-stillness. Then the water trickling down the sides of the stairs increased to a steady stream an inch deep from wall to wall, waterfalling into the coal room in dirty little cascades.

"What the hell?" Patrick breathed.

From upstairs came the sound of screaming.

Jonathan and Gregory dropped their shovels and all three boys tore up the stairs at a run.

"Wait!" Patrick called. "Don't leave me down here!"

But they were already gone, up the stairs and through the kitchen and into the dining room.

The room was in chaos. The storm, which had already seemed impossibly fierce, was doubled in strength and fury. All the windows had blown out, every single one, and the door was ripped off its hinges, leaving one whole wall open to the raging wind and rain. All the candles were out, leaving the room in darkness except when it was lit by flashes of lightning. The boys were all huddled behind tables.

Jonathan, Roger, and Gregory stopped in their tracks. The water in the room was no longer an inch deep—it was over their ankles, and rising.

"Look at that!" Miguel shouted over the thundering storm. "In the courtyard!"

Ducking heads peeked from behind the tables. Jonathan's eyes peered through the pelting rain into the darkness beyond the glassless windows. For a moment, there was only wet, howling blackness.

Then a bright white strobe of lightning lit the scene, and he saw it.

A boat, drifting in the courtyard. Sailing and bobbing right in the middle of the school.

Jonathan and Sebastian and a few others ran to the windows, standing a couple of cautious steps back and squinting into the darkness outside.

Lightning flashed again.

"It's empty!"

"That's the mail boat. The one the guy came in."

"The gate must have blown open!"

Jonathan looked down the row of terrified faces.

"It's floating out there," he said. "There's enough water inside for it to float."

They looked out at the boat, rocking its way through the storm toward them, rising and falling with the waves.

"It ain't just puddles out there," Walter said.

"It's flooded. The island's underwater."

They looked down at the water, now above their ankles.

From behind them came a wrenching, shrieking sound, followed by a thunderous bang. It rang out from the doorway that led into Slabhenge and for a moment overpowered even the sound of the storm raging around them.

Jonathan splashed through the water to the doorway. He took one step into the lightless corridor and listened. He heard echoes of banging, and rushing, and a wet slurping roar.

"It's the Hatch!" he screamed, the wind whipping the words out of his mouth. "It opened!"

CHAPTER TWENTY-SIX
GOING ALONE

The boys came out from behind and under the tables. They gathered in the middle of the room, feeling for each other in the darkness. A few were crying. Questions were shouted by shaking voices.

"Everyone settle down!" Sebastian's harsh command silenced the rising voices. "Just shut up, everyone! Let me think! We're all fine!"

His words shook Jonathan with a realization.

"All!? What about Colin! He's lower down than we are! We have to go save him!"

Sebastian shook his head.

"No way! We're not going past that Hatch if it's open!"

"We have to! He'll drown!"

"So will we if we go after him. We're staying right here until the storm stops. We can sit up on the tables."

"No, Sebastian, we have to—"

"No, Johnny. We can't save him." Sebastian's voice was as hard as the sword glinting in his hand. "We're not gonna die trying."

Jonathan swallowed. His whole body was trembling. With cold. With anger. With fear. He rubbed his arms with shivering hands, feeling the burns and scars through his wet sleeves. He imagined he could hear Colin crying for help. In his mind he saw soggy, water-ruined paper birds. Rain-soaked flowers.

"I'm going," he said, and his voice was soft but at least as hard as Sebastian's.

Sebastian blinked and breathed hard through his nose. His jaw muscles rippled.

"Fine. But you're going alone. And you can't save him."

"Yes, I can."

"Don't go!" Tony said.

"Don't do it, man," Walter pleaded.

"It's crazy!" Gerald yelled. The water was halfway up their calves now.

"Let me have a lantern," Jonathan said into Sebastian's eyes. Sebastian glanced quickly around.

"We only have three left." Sebastian said. Jonathan kept his eyes locked on Sebastian's, unblinking. After a moment, Sebastian blinked. "Fine. Take one. Better bring a candle, too."

Without another word, Jonathan jerked a lantern out of the nearest kid's hand. He yanked a candle out of the holder by the doorway. He was two steps into the corridor when a sudden thought stopped him.

"Patrick!" he exclaimed. "The coal room is flooding." He looked to Roger and Gregory. They didn't look tough at all. They looked soaking wet and scared. "Go get him and bring him up."

The two boys didn't move, except to look at Sebastian. After a moment, he nodded. They turned and jogged toward the coal room.

Jonathan adjusted his grip on the lantern's slippery handle and took off into the darkness as fast as he could through the rising water.

"Good luck!" Walter shouted after him. Then another kid shouted the same thing. As he sprinted around the first corner and out of earshot, Jonathan heard a chorus of scared voices shouting the same thing. Their voices echoed behind him, following him into the black, flooded maze of Slabhenge.

"Good luck!"

CHAPTER TWENTY-SEVEN
DARKNESS AND DROWNING

As he ran, Jonathan tried to retrace in his mind the path they'd taken when they'd returned from leaving Colin to the rats and shadows. Rising up was all he remembered clearly. And passing the Hatch. He made his way there, holding the lantern out in front of him.

He ducked under the rope and started down the stairs, then cried out and slid to a stop.

Three steps down, the stairs disappeared into black, bubbling water.

The lantern nearly slipped from his fingers. He caught it and fell against the stone wall, panting.

The Hatch *had* cracked open. And the ocean it had been holding back had broken out of the dungeon.

He held the lantern out. He could just see, through the water, where the ceiling flattened out above the landing, now lost under murky seawater.

"I can make it," he told himself. His voice sounded tiny and hollow in the echoing gurgles of the flooded stairwell. "Just a quick swim down, then up." There was an iron hook on the wall by his hand and he hung the lantern on it. He felt in his pockets and pulled out the book of matches that Sebastian had given him earlier, when he'd first sent him out to join Colin. It had been only a few hours before. It felt like forever.

He spit and blew, drying out his mouth. Then he tucked the book of matches into his mouth and closed his lips tight, holding the matches on his tongue. Clutching the candle in his hand, he dove into the dark water before his fear could get strong enough to stop him.

The water was freezing. His muscles tightened and shook and he almost turned around, but he shook his head and kept going. He kept his eyes open and the chilled, salty water burned. He swam with his arms and kicked with his legs and the light from his hanging lantern got dimmer and darker and more distant and then it was all the way gone. Jonathan swam through freezing blackness. He tried not to think of the skull that rolled and knocked somewhere in the dark water there with him.

Down he swam, under the ceiling ledge. He stayed near the top, bumping and scraping on the rough ceiling stones. The water wasn't still; it swelled and moved with currents and surges, no doubt coursing in and out through the Hatch with the rise and fall of the waves in the storm outside.

He swam along the level landing ceiling, his lungs beginning to burn. His lips were pressed together as hard as he could to keep the matches dry. A strong surge of water from below crushed him against the ceiling and pushed him back. He fought against it, digging his elbow into the corner where the wall and ceiling met, then kicked on desperately.

Finally, he felt the ceiling begin to slope upward. He was

swimming up the far staircase. It suddenly occurred to him that he had no guarantee that the far side was above water. Maybe the other side of Slabhenge was all already underwater. Maybe he would swim up and up without ever finding air and then drown in some dark and flooded corridor, a book of matches in his mouth.

But at last his head broke the surface and he gave a final kick and gasped a mouthful of cold, delicious air. His feet found the stairs beneath him and he stumbled up, out of the water. He staggered, dripping and shaking out of the stairwell and into the hallway.

He was in utter blackness. Just like the first time he'd come here, when he'd dropped his lantern by the Hatch. He shook the water off his hand and pulled the matches out of his mouth.

The hallway was filled with the wet sounds of storm and flood. His gasping lungs added their own noise. His hands shook as he struck the first match.

It lit, a beautiful yellow flame in all that looming darkness. He smiled and held it to the candle's wick.

Nothing happened. He kept holding it, waiting for the flame to grow and the wick to take light. But the match burned down to his fingers and then out.

"Damn it," he cursed, his voice tight with shivering. "Of course, idiot. The wick's wet."

He struck another one and held it to the wick. Eventually, he told himself, the flames would dry the wick. And then it would light. He had to believe that.

He didn't have time to wait. Colin could already be underwater. If he wasn't yet, he would be soon. He stepped cautiously forward, his eyes darting from his feet to the flame and wick in his hands.

The second match burned down. He held it until it singed his fingertips, then stopped to light another.

On the fourth match, the wick lit. Weakly at first, a bare little blue ball of flame clinging to the candle's tip. Then it grew and strengthened and stretched into a tall, bright finger of flame. He held his hand in front of it to keep it from blowing out and sped his steps to a jog.

The path came back to him. A familiar corner passed, then a stairwell he was pretty sure he remembered climbing up, then a twisting little passageway he was almost certain they'd filed through. He was close.

He dropped down a short staircase and stopped.

The water was here. Up to his knees. And he was pretty sure that Colin's room was another staircase lower. Up ahead, he heard a waterfall. No, he thought, not a waterfall. The sound of freezing water pouring down a stone staircase. He ran toward the sound, the deepening water pushing back at him.

"Colin!" he screamed. "Colin! Can you hear me?"

"Jonathan?"

Jonathan almost collapsed in relief when he heard the familiar voice answer him.

"Hurry! I'm almotht under!"

Jonathan ran to the staircase. Water was gushing over the edge, bubbling and frothing. He leapt down the stairs, pushed along by the river of water, and came to a splashing stop at the bottom, his head going under but his arm stretched high to keep the candle out of the water.

He quickly got his footing. The water came up to his waist.

Colin's head and neck were all that stuck up above the water. His eyes were wide and terrified. The water was rising fast enough to see it; even as Jonathan stood there, frozen with fear, it rose and lapped at Colin's chin.

"Untie me!" he begged, his voice high and panicked. "Hurry! Pleath!"

Jonathan hurried over, the water sloshing around his belly button. The ropes were underwater. He looked at his candle, then into Colin's eyes.

"We're gonna have to get out of here in the dark," he said.

Colin was stretching his neck up, the water now splashing against his mouth.

"Fine!" he gurgled. "Hurry!"

Jonathan dropped the candle and matches. The room was plunged into darkness.

His fingers fumbled under the water. They were cold and stiff. He found the ropes and pulled at them, jerking and tugging. They were tight and wet, swollen even tighter by the water. He worked his fingers into one of the loops and managed to pull it loose. He began tugging at another loop.

"Hurry u—" Colin started to beg, before his words were cut off by a wet gurgle.

"Colin?"

There was no answer, except a frantic moaning. Jonathan lifted one hand and felt in the darkness for Colin's face. The water was above his mouth now. His head was tilted back so that his nose just barely rose above the waterline.

Jonathan yanked and wrestled frantically with the knots. There was a surge of water. He felt the water level rise suddenly, up to his stooped shoulder. Colin's moans grew more desperate, but quieter. Jonathan felt with his hand again.

The water had risen over Colin's face.

He let go of the ropes and wrapped his arms around Colin's bound body. With all his strength he lifted him, chair and all, above the water. He heard Colin gasp and cough. The water was still rising. It was to Jonathan's ribs now.

"I'm gonna have to put you back down now," he said. "Take a deep breath." Colin sucked in a great gasping breath. Jonathan dropped him and reached for the ropes. Colin's whole head was underwater, and the ropes were too deep for Jonathan to reach without going under himself. He gulped a huge lungful of air and ducked beneath the surface.

He loosened another loop. Then another. He pulled a long stretch of rope through. The rope was mostly slack now, with one stubborn knot left tight against Colin's wrists. He pulled and tugged and got one loop loose before he ran out of air. He could feel Colin kicking and fighting in the water.

Jonathan wrapped his arms around Colin and picked him up again.

They both panted and gasped and choked. The water was to Jonathan's shoulders.

"This is it," he said. "I'll get it this time."

"You have to," Colin sputtered.

"I will." Jonathan readied himself for another drop into the water.

"Jonathan!" Colin said quickly, stopping him. "If you can't get it, jutht go. You can make it out yourthelf."

Jonathan took a couple more heaving breaths.

"Shut up, Colin. And take a deep breath."

They dropped together beneath the surface.

CHAPTER TWENTY-EIGHT
SAVED

The ropes were stubborn. The water was cold, and dark, and determined. Colin fought and thrashed against his ties. His closed-mouth screaming rang dull and frantic under the black water.

Jonathan's fingers and arms burned with exhaustion. His lungs screamed for air.

He felt the burning in his arms and gritted his teeth. His lungs begged him to swim to the surface, to air, but he held tight to the ropes and worked at the knots.

I can do it, he told himself. Even his mind's voice was breathless and terrified. *I can save her!* He shook his head and slid his fingers between the taut ropes. *I can save him*, he corrected himself. *I can.*

His fingers slid through. He hooked them around the last loop and pulled. It hung for a moment, stuck, then slid loose and the rope went slack and Colin shook his arms free and they both kicked up to the surface.

They tread water for a few ravenous breaths. He'd done it. He'd saved him. Tears were hot in Jonathan's eyes. He wasn't sure why. Relief, maybe.

His head bumped something hard and he jerked when he realized it was the ceiling.

"We've gotta get out of here!" he shouted. "Follow me."

They swam through the complete blackness toward the doorway. The water was still flowing down the staircase, pushing them back into the room, trapping them in the rising water.

"Grab the wall with your fingers!" he hollered over his shoulder. "You can hold on to the cracks between the blocks!"

He pulled himself block by block up the staircase, against the current, kicking with his legs. His fingers and arms ached but he made it, finally hooking his hands around the edge of the upper doorway. The water was only shoulder deep there and he was able to brace his feet against the doorway and help pull Colin into the corridor.

They stood for just a moment to catch their breath.

"Do you know how to get back?" Colin asked. "Without any light?"

"I think so." Jonathan started off, wading through the water, feeling the walls with his fingers.

"Hey," Colin said, reaching out to stop him. "Thankth for coming back for me. For thaving me."

"No problem." Jonathan thought about the swim still ahead, past the Hatch. The water was even higher now. "But I'd save your thanks. We're not out of the woods yet."

They made their way through the twisting blackness. Jonathan ran through the mental map in his mind, retracing the path he'd taken three times now, negotiating turns and stairwells and pitch-black hallways. As they rose, the water got more shallow. Eventually, they could move quickly, with the water only splashing around their ankles.

Jonathan led them confidently down a corridor and started to turn, then stopped. Colin bumped into his back.

"Wait," he said. "I need to warn him."

"Warn who?"

Jonathan chewed on his lip. The water was still rising. Time was running out. They needed to get back. But he knew he had to.

"Follow me," he said, and then turned and walked the other way. He knew exactly where he was now and he moved quickly, anticipating stairs before he got to them and turning corners confidently. Colin struggled to keep up.

"Where are we going?"

Jonathan stopped, gasping for breath. He could hear, all around him, rats splashing and flailing in the briny floodwaters.

"There," he answered, pointing up ahead at the thin line of light gleaming just below the water, shining from under a closed door.

They jogged forward and Jonathan knocked urgently on the door.

It swung open.

"Ah," the librarian said. "You've come back." His hair was wet, stuck down to his head and over his face in a stringy mess. Wind whistled in the room behind him, tossing a blizzard of pages and papers around in the air. Ninety-Nine shivered on his shoulder, his pink tail dangling down the old man's chest. Even soaking wet, the rat looked huge. Colin gasped and took a step back.

"Please. Come in. We can find you. Another book."

CHAPTER TWENTY-NINE
A LUNATIC (NOT AN IDIOT)

The library, always so neat and dry and dustless, was in shambles.

The storm had shattered the windows here, too. Rain and wind howled and blustered inside, soaking the books and ripping out pages and leaving puddles on the floor and bookshelves.

"We've gotta go," Jonathan blurted out, taking a step inside. "And you've got to come with us."

"Oh," the librarian answered calmly, turning and walking slowly into his wrecked library. "I don't. Think so. What kind of book. Would you like?"

"No, *really*, we've all gotta go. This is a hurricane. The whole place is flooded. The island's going under."

The librarian stopped. He turned and looked at Jonathan in his hunched, twisted way. A small smile rose, just barely, to his lips.

"Yes," he replied. "I know. It's the sea. Come at last. To claim her own."

"Then come on! We've got to get out! To higher ground!"

The librarian chuckled.

"Yes," he said. "You do. The sea. Is coming." He reached up and stroked Ninety-Nine's dripping fur. "But I. Am staying."

"You'll die," Jonathan insisted.

The librarian shrugged.

"I have lived. Long enough. I have never left. This island. Where else. Would I go?"

Jonathan shook his head and stammered.

"No . . . but . . . but . . ."

The librarian turned and looked out at the storm through his narrow, shattered windows.

"You must take the other boys. Higher. To the only part of Slabhenge. That will last."

"What? Where is that?"

"The old lighthouse. Up, up. Up. Above the Admiral's room. The lighthouse was here. First. Before the asylum. Before the school. It is built on the original stone. The true stone. Of the old island. The rest"—the librarian spread his arms to include the windswept stone structure around him—"the rest is all built on sand. But the lighthouse. Will stand."

"Come on, Jonathan," Colin whispered behind him. "We have to go."

Jonathan cocked his head. There was something the librarian had said that stuck in his mind. *You must take the other boys.*

"You know," he said, looking the librarian in the eyes. "You know about the Admiral. About the grown-ups."

The man's small smile grew just a bit.

"I am a lunatic. Not an idiot. I go at night. To the kitchen. It's been terribly messy." The librarian paused, working his fingers into Ninety-Nine's fur. Ninety-Nine closed his eyes and leaned back into the scratching finger. "And ice cream is my favorite food. It's kept. In the freezer. Of course."

"We didn't kill them. It was lightning. They were all outside, standing in a puddle. The Admiral had his sword in the air."

"Hmm," the librarian said thoughtfully. "The Admiral *was* a madman. Standing around in a puddle. Holding a metal sword in the air. During a lightning storm." He pursed his lips and shrugged. "Sounds about right. For him."

The librarian nodded, then looked to the nearest shelf. "Now. You must go. Quickly. So we need to choose. A book."

"No, I—can't really take one. We have to swim to get back. It'll get wet."

The librarian clucked his tongue, his eyes still on the books' spines.

"All of these books. Will be at the bottom of the sea. Very soon. And you cannot leave a library. Without a book. Ah. Here. This one."

The old man pulled a book off the shelf. It was thick and bound in soft black leather.

"*Moby-Dick*. The story of a madman. Lost at sea. He dies in a storm. The hero is the only one who lives." The librarian handed the book to Jonathan and squinted up sideways at him. "I don't think. That is what will happen here. No. You will save them, Jonathan. Now go. To the lighthouse."

Jonathan breathed quickly through his nose.

"Are you sure—"

"Oh. Yes. Go."

Jonathan looked into the librarian's eyes.

"Thank you," he said.

"Mmm."

Jonathan turned to go.

"Wait. There is one thing. You could do. For me."

"What?"

The librarian reached up and plucked the monstrous rat from his shoulder. He pressed his lips for a long moment into the rodent's neck, then held him out with two hands toward Jonathan.

"Take Ninety-Nine. With you. You could save him. Like the others."

Jonathan gulped. The rat looked at him with curious, shiny eyes. He didn't hiss or snarl.

Jonathan handed *Moby-Dick* to Colin and reached out reluctantly to take the offered animal. Ninety-Nine was surprisingly soft. And predictably heavy.

The rat sniffed for a second at Jonathan's hands, then scrambled gently up to perch on his shoulder.

The librarian watched. His eyes were wet and glowing.

"Yes," he said. "You can save him. And maybe. When you're home. Find him a wife."

Jonathan nodded.

"Sure. A nice big wife."

"Yes. That's right. Now. Off you go. Take a candle. I won't. Be needing them."

Colin grabbed a candle from atop the closest bookshelf and the two boys ran out into the corridor. Jonathan looked back once to see the librarian standing in the doorway with the door wide open. He was lit from behind by a few flickering candles, his hair whipped about by the wind. Rats were swarming through the open door by his feet, seeking the light and relative dryness of the library. Several of them had no tails. The old man made no move to stop them. He wouldn't die alone.

Jonathan followed the light of Colin's candle through the hallways. The water was above their ankles. They arrived panting at the stairs that led down past the Hatch. The water was much higher now than it had been when Jonathan came before. It was rising and falling and swirling, lapping at the very top step. It would be a longer swim this time. And now he had a rat.

"What do we do?"

"We swim, Colin. That's how I got through. Just a quick dip, down and then up again. No big deal."

"What about the candle?"

"Don't worry about it. There's a lit lantern on the other side. Just take a deep breath."

Jonathan handed Ninety-Nine over before Colin could think to push it away. He dropped *Moby-Dick* with a splash at his feet.

"I can't believe I'm doing this," Jonathan said. He tucked his shirt into his pants tightly, then unbuttoned the top two buttons. Taking the rat back from Colin, he slid him into his shirt against his bare skin. He rebuttoned his shirt. The rat scratched and writhed against his body, squeaking and squirming.

"Come on. Before he chews through my stomach."

Without thinking Jonathan dove headfirst, pushing off the top step as hard as he could to rocket himself through the water. As soon as the cold water hit them, Ninety-Nine went crazy. He tore and fought and twisted. Jonathan gritted his teeth and swam as hard as he could, pawing and kicking at the black water. He didn't slow down when an upwelling of water pressed him against the ceiling. He didn't slow when the rat's teeth sank into his skin. He didn't slow when he saw, through the salty murk, the glow of lantern light up ahead. He didn't slow until his feet found the far stairs and his head broke into air and he stepped up out of the water.

He climbed a few steps up. Ninety-Nine was shaking and coughing inside his shirt. He struggled weakly against the wet fabric. Jonathan unbuttoned his shirt and pulled the bedraggled rat out. Ninety-Nine coughed up some water and then slowly crawled back up to Jonathan's shoulder, his body shaking. Jonathan gave him a reassuring scratch.

Colin's head popped up into the stairwell, gasping for air. Jonathan helped him up the slippery stairs, pulling the lantern from the hook.

They stood panting, eyes on the dark water they'd emerged from.

"Well," Colin gasped. "That wathn't tho—"

His words were cut off by a wrenching, grating crack from below the water's surface. A great rush of huge bubbles rose to the surface, and with a sickening whoosh, the water began to rise more quickly. So quickly they could see it climbing and racing up the stairs in a rapid, steady surge.

"What happened?" Colin cried, stumbling backward up the stairs.

"I don't know! I think something else just broke open! We gotta go!"

The water rose up the stairs faster than they could climb, nearly overtaking them before they reached the top. By the time they broke out into the hallway, the water was a surging wave that came nearly to their waists.

Together they ran through the familiar hallways they both knew, winding back toward the dining room. The dark wall of water gurgled just behind them, slurping at the walls and sloshing around corners. Ninety-Nine clung to Jonathan's shoulders with a firm grip of his claws. His tail slapped on Jonathan's back as they ran.

They burst into the dining room just ahead of the wave.

They almost ran into Sebastian and the rest of the boys. They were all crowded around the door, holding lanterns and candles. Sebastian was at the front, his sword out in front of him and a coil of rope thrown over his shoulder, a dark look on his face.

CHAPTER THIRTY
HOME

The wave of water was slowed when it hit the narrow doorway. It crested and poured into the dining room, a frothy white head of bubbles at its top. Colin and Jonathan braced themselves as it hit their backs. Some of the boys who weren't ready were knocked off their feet and sent tumbling head over heels in the water.

The water pouring in from the doorway leveled out as the water in the room rose, until it all stood flat, above their knees. And still slowly rising. The boys regathered themselves, coughing and rubbing the water out of their eyes.

Sebastian had never lost his footing. He still stood with his sword, eyes on Jonathan.

"We were just about to leave," he said.

"Where were you guys going?"

Sebastian looked him in the eye.

"We were coming to find you."

"Really?"

Sebastian shrugged and nodded.

"Yeah."

"Oh. Thanks."

Sebastian shrugged again, then squinted and looked closer at Jonathan. "Jesus! What is that thing on your shoulder?"

"It's a rat. Don't worry about it. We gotta go. Quick. Or we're all gonna die."

"Go where?"

"To the lighthouse."

"What lighthouse?"

"I'll explain as we go. We've gotta move."

Jonathan started to brush past him, but Sebastian put a hand out and stopped him. Forcefully.

"Easy, Johnny. I didn't want to get blamed for you dying. Doesn't mean I want you in charge. We decided to stay here, where it's safe."

"It isn't safe here, Sebastian. This whole place is going under. The water's rising. And the island is sinking. We've got to go. Up."

"Up? It's safer down here," Sebastian insisted.

"What if the tower blows over?" Gerald asked.

"What if lightning hits it?" Francis demanded.

"Going up is our only choice!" Jonathan insisted. "It's the only way to save ourselves."

"You can't trust him!" Benny's voice was ugly and hissing. "You know what he's here for!"

Lightning flashed through the windows. The wind was a roar, swirling around them. Jonathan saw the boys' faces harden at Benny's words, saw the doubt flicker in their eyes.

"You're wrong, Benny!" Jonathan said, his voice rising with the pounding of his heart and the raging of the storm. "You *can* trust me! My sister . . . she . . . she *did* die in a fire, and . . . but . . ." Jonathan stopped, his voice choked by tears.

"But you didn't thtart it," Colin finished. "Did you?"

"Stop it, Colin," Jonathan said.

But Colin didn't stop.

"You told me, Jonathan. You told me she took your matcheth."

Jonathan swallowed. Took a choking breath. He looked into Colin's face. Colin's eyes widened.

"Oh," he breathed. "It wath *her*, wathn't it? Your thithter thtarted the fire."

"Shut up, Colin."

"And you took the blame. You let them think it wath you. Becauth—"

"Because it's my fault!" Jonathan interrupted, shouting. "They were my matches! She learned from me!" Jonathan's voice broke off, his shoulders shaking with sobs. Ninety-Nine's claws dug in harder to stay on. Jonathan closed his eyes against his tears and lowered his head. "It's my fault."

He heard, through the storm and his own sadness, the sound of someone splashing toward him. Two hands, gentle as birds, came to rest on his arm. They worked at the buttons of his sleeves, then pulled the fabric up to his elbows. Jonathan didn't fight.

"How did you get the thcars?" Colin asked.

Jonathan didn't answer.

"How did you get the thcars?" Colin asked again. Then, in a whisper so low only Jonathan could hear it, he added, "Tell them, Jonathan. If you tell them, they'll believe you. They'll follow you. You can thave them."

Jonathan took one breath. Then two. He opened his eyes. He lifted his head.

"I didn't start the fire," he said. The words came out scratchy and faint. He cleared his throat and started again, his voice ringing clear into the faces of the lost boys around him, and into his own ears. "I didn't start the fire. I woke up. And I heard her screaming. And I ran downstairs. But . . . the fire was too big. Too hot. I couldn't get to her. I tried. I tried so hard." He held up his arms. The scar tissue, twisted and tough, flashed whitely in the lightning. "I tried until the firefighters got there and dragged me away. I did every-thing I could to save her." He realized he was shouting, as much to himself as to the watching boys. "I did everything I could!"

Tears joined the seawater on his face. Warm tears, clean and true.

Walter walked up to him and put a hand on his shoulder.

"It's okay, man," he said. "It's okay."

Jonathan took a long, steadying breath. He nodded a thank-you to Walter, and to Colin. Then he looked up at all the other boys. The Scars.

"We've got to get to the only part of this place that's built on rock. The only part that isn't going to wash away. We've got to get to the old lighthouse."

His words hung like a tattered flag in the wind-swept room.

"He's telling the truth," a deep voice interjected. They all turned and looked to where Patrick sat, still tied to his chair but now atop one of the dining room tables. "About the lighthouse. There did used to be one here. Going way back now, to the old sailing days. It's built on the stones, indeed."

Jonathan looked at Sebastian.

"We need to go, Sebastian."

Sebastian's jaw was clenched. His chest was heaving with shallow breaths. He looked down to the water around his thighs, then up at Patrick.

"What about your boat?" he asked.

Patrick shook his head.

"No way. Too late for that. I barely made it out here, and the storm's only gotten stronger."

Sebastian bit at his lip. His eyes cut to Jonathan. He nodded.

Jonathan blew out a deep breath. He nodded back. Then he turned to Roger and Gregory.

"Cut him loose," he said. "And all of you, follow me."

Without waiting for an answer, Jonathan waded through the waist-deep water past Sebastian, past the waiting boys, toward the staircase that led up toward Sebastian's room. The Admiral's room. The lighthouse.

Colin followed him. Ninety-Nine clung to Jonathan's shoulder.

When he got to the stairwell, he stopped and turned. The boys were filing after him. All of them. They looked lost and frightened in the raging wind and the flashbulb lightning. They were drenched and exhausted and terrified. They needed to be saved.

Sebastian was up on the table. Sawing at Patrick's ropes with his sword. He didn't look terrifying. He looked like a confused kid, finding his way through the dark.

Jonathan felt something bump him, and looked down. It was a piece of the ruined Sinner's Sorrow, bobbing in the water. Several more pieces floated around him. He picked up a piece.

"Everyone grab a piece," he said. "We're gonna need the wood."

The storm was like a beast hammering at Slabhenge. Even running up the stone stairwell, they could hear it outside, through the walls, howling to be let in.

Jonathan ran past the doors to the grown-ups' rooms, past the locked door to the Admiral's office, to the far, dark end of the hall. The end of the hallway was a curved wall, crumbling with age. It was made of a different stone than the rest of Slabhenge. Bigger blocks of grayer rock, rock that looked even older than the rock Jonathan had grown used to being surrounded by.

In the curved wall of ancient stone was a door made of tremendously thick slats of dark wood bound together with rusty iron. The door looked like it hadn't been opened in years. Instead of a knob, it simply had a metal latch, like a pirate's treasure chest, that connected to a bolt on the stone wall. Jonathan yanked on the latch, and it opened with a protesting creak of rusty metal that had been wet and unused for too long. He pushed on the door and it swung slowly open.

Beyond the door was a round stairwell, leading up in one direction and down in the other. Its walls and stairs were made of the same gray rock. The air smelled stale. Dusty. Forgotten. It was even colder in the stairwell than it was in the rest of the school.

The boys piled up behind Jonathan.

"Up," he said. "We've got to go up."

They raced up the stairs, taking them two at a time. Round and round the stairwell spiraled, up and up through dank darkness, with all the dark world raging outside the walls.

Jonathan reached the top breathless. Colin was behind him, then the rest. Sebastian was the last, behind Patrick.

The top of the tower was a round room. On all sides were windows, sturdy double-paned glass crisscrossed by metal bars. The lightning filled the sky all around them. They were surrounded by the storm, teetering in the angry heavens. On all sides were windows to the black clouds and whipping wind and sideways rain.

In the middle of the room, on a raised stone landing, was a great black iron bowl, big enough for Jonathan to have stretched out and lain down in. A massive curved mirror stood on the far side of the bowl, mounted on a mechanism of gears and bars and wheels that circled the bowl. To Jonathan's right was a large metal handle.

"The lighthouse," Jonathan whispered. "Just like he said."

The boys stood in silence, looking out the windows at the hurricane that raged all around them, inches away. It was almost deafening.

They could see all of Slabhenge when the lightning flashed. The courtyard, flooded now halfway up the windows into the dining room. The boat still rocked between the walls.

They could see the roof that covered the rest of the school, rising and falling with the confusing ramblings of the mazelike building. They could see the other towers poking stubbornly up into the black skies.

"Look!" Miguel shouted over the storm. "Look at the towers!"

They all crowded to the windows.

"What?"

"What about them?"

"There's only three! One's missing!"

They all looked and saw it then. The far tower was gone. Simply gone. They could see where the stone walls led to the space that it should occupy, but the walls stopped in a jagged, sawtooth break. A loose pile of stones was all that remained of the tower, avalanching down into the white-capped sea.

Jonathan looked at Colin. Colin was staring at the pile of

rubble with wide eyes. It was Colin's tower. The tower with his mattress and his papers and his three lonely candlesticks. Somewhere among those waves bobbed dozens of white paper cranes. And a few shiny gold chocolate wrappers.

"There! Look at the gate!"

They all spun back to the courtyard with its ghostly boat. The far side, with the watery stairs and the gate through which they had all entered Slabhenge, was crumbling before their eyes. The arch above the gate crashed into the water with a massive splash. The gigantic waves poured relentlessly through the gap, pushing and pulling at the hundred-year-old walls. They fell apart, stone block by stone block, as the water coursed through. Soon the whole wall was gone, a heaped mound of stones just below the water's surface. The courtyard was left with walls on only three sides.

With the one wall gone, the waves rushed unhindered into the courtyard, rising above the level of the dining room windows. It wouldn't be long before the rest of the walls succumbed to the ravenous, storm-fueled waters of the sea.

"The whole dining room's under now," Walter said, his voice hollow with shock.

"The kitchen," Tony said.

"The freezer," David added. They all stood and stared.

"We should light the lighthouse," Jonathan said, watching Slabhenge fall apart. No one heard him over the wind and the thunder and their own openmouthed amazement.

"We should light the lighthouse!" Jonathan shouted, and stricken faces turned toward him.

"Why?"

"So they know we're here!" he answered. "So they send help!" He looked into Colin's eyes, then Walter's, then Patrick's. "I want to go home." His voice cracked at the end and got lost in the mad confusion of noise. He said it again, from the bottom of his lungs. "I want to go home!"

"If ye light it, they'll know to come!" Patrick yelled from behind them. "When they can, anyway! This old thing ain't been fired up since before I was born! They'll notice it for sure, and they'll know to come!"

Jonathan ran to a large wooden bin that lined one of the walls and threw open the lid with all his strength.

Inside, neatly stacked, were rows of split logs. Firewood. Stowed, dry and safe. By a man who began as a madhouse baby and ended as a forgotten librarian. In between, though, he was a lighthouse keeper.

"We need paper!" he shouted, turning to face the group.

"The school office is underwater by now!" Benny yelled back.

"What about the Admiral's room?"

They all looked at Sebastian. He shook his head.

"None in there! He didn't even have a book!"

Jonathan's mind flashed. "The Admiral's office!"

"It's locked, remember?"

Jonathan smiled. He reached into his pocket and pulled out the rusty metal key that had fallen out of the dead Admiral's jacket. Sebastian's mouth dropped open.

"Come on," Jonathan said to him, tossing his piece of the Sinner's Sorrow into the great iron bowl. "The rest of you, get the wood in the fire pit!" He took the lantern from Colin, then pulled Ninety-Nine gently from his shoulder and handed him to Colin. Colin grimaced and held him with two hands, out away from his body.

Jonathan and Sebastian ran back down the lighthouse stairs. When they got to the old door, Jonathan swore.

There was an inch of water running like a river down the stairwell, pouring in from the hallway. The water was even higher than he'd imagined. It was already to the second story.

"We've gotta hurry," he said to Sebastian. "This whole place is gonna fill up and fall down."

They bolted down the hall, their feet splashing through the rushing water. At the door to the Admiral's office, Jonathan held the lantern up and stabbed the key into the lock. It clicked into place. Then turned. He shouldered the door open and they ran inside. The water rushed in with them.

The office was lost in shadows, but Jonathan remembered it vividly from that first, awful night. The Admiral's sneering voice, his demonic eyebrows. The pain of the Sinner's Sorrow. The letter home, full of lies. The Admiral's acidic words as he'd read Jonathan's paperwork: *You have done terrible things, haven't you, Jonathan Grisby?*

Jonathan walked straight over to the standing file behind the desk where he'd seen the Admiral tuck his folder. He pulled it open. Inside were neatly ordered, identical manila folders, each stuffed with papers. He didn't have to count to know there were sixteen files. On the tab of the first folder was scrawled his own name. His eyes scanned the rest. *Colin Kerrigan. Sebastian Mortimer.* And thirteen more.

He set the lantern down and grabbed half of the folders, then handed them to Sebastian. He tucked the other half under his arm and picked up the lantern.

"This should be enough," he said, and they darted back out into the hallway. The water was even higher now. Jonathan winced and dodged a dead rat being washed down the hallway. Another one bobbed by, paws stuck out stiff into the air.

At the top of the lighthouse, the other boys and Patrick had half the wood piled in the big metal bowl with the ravaged remains of the Sinner's Sorrow. They stood waiting on the raised platform around it, looking out at the world gone mad. Jonathan glanced quickly and counted the towers. Another had fallen. Only two were still standing. And the lighthouse. Another of the courtyard's walls was mostly gone.

Jonathan looked at the name on the top file in his hands. *Walter Holcomb.* He handed the folder to Walter. *Reginald*

Miller the next one said, and he gave it to Reggie. Sebastian started to do the same.

Eventually, Jonathan was left with one folder in his hands. *Jonathan Grisby*, it said. He opened it and words from the top page jumped out at him. *Guilty. Criminal. Arson.* He ground his teeth together and crumpled the paper into a ball. He stepped forward and shoved it under the waiting pile of wood.

He looked at the second sheet. More words swam up through the darkness and lightning. *Death. Sophia. Injuries. Grief. Guilt.* Tears scalded his eyes. His lungs shivered as they breathed.

He wadded the paper up into a tight ball. As tight as his fists could manage. And he added it to the unlit fire.

Around him, other boys started to do the same. Amidst the roar of wind and storm came the sound of ripping paper, of crumpling files. And all around the circle, fuel was added to the lighthouse fire.

Eventually, they all stood, hands clean and empty. Beneath the ready logs was tucked a white mound of twisted paper. A crumpled pile of crimes. A bonfire's worth of guilt and punishment and dark history.

Sebastian took a candle from another boy's hand. He leaned forward. But he stopped, the candle's flame inches from the paper.

He frowned. He leaned back. He looked at Jonathan. Lightning flickered, showing his flooded eyes.

"I don't want to go," he said.

Jonathan blinked and didn't answer.

"You wanna know why I never wrote letters?" Sebastian asked. "Because there was no one to send them to. I got no parents. I got no family. I've spent my whole life in places like this. Or orphanages. Group homes. Foster homes." He looked out at the storm that was pressed in all around them, screaming and pounding the windows. "I don't have anyone to read my letters. No one cares. I got no one to write to."

Jonathan swallowed and took a step closer to Sebastian.

"You can write to me," he said.

Sebastian's eyebrows furrowed. His mouth opened, but he didn't say anything.

"You can write to me," Gerald said.

"You can write to me, man," Walter called out.

"You can write to me, Thebathtian," Colin said, just loud enough to be heard.

Sebastian sniffed. He nodded, looking around, then rubbed his eyes with his sleeve.

"Light the fire," Jonathan said. Sebastian nodded again, one more small nod, then stretched the candle out and touched it to the nearest paper. Other boys stepped forward then with their own candles, holding the flames to the papers closest to themselves.

Climbing fingers of flames crept up through the criss-crossed wood. The papers flared and burned into bright flashes of yellow. The boys stepped back and covered their eyes.

There was a crackle and a snap as a piece of wood caught fire. A couple of wisping sparks rose up and flickered out.

The sound of the fire grew louder, the light brighter, the flames higher, the heat hotter. The boys stepped down from the platform and back to the lower floor. The room grew warm. Their soaking clothes steamed in the heat.

With a final flurry of crackling, the whole pile caught fire. Flames arced and danced six feet high. The round room, hemmed in on all sides by the stormy world's fury, grew brighter than daylight. Jonathan stepped to the metal hand crank and muscled it into motion. With a shuddering, squeaking creak the gears and wheels attached to the mirror sprang to reluctant life. The mirror began to slowly rotate around the towering flames of their signal fire, magnifying and reflecting the light out into the clouds, the storm, the world.

Sebastian joined him at the crank and they worked together. The mirror moved faster, sending its spear of light out into the darkness.

After a while, Jonathan let go and stepped back, sweating and gasping. Another boy took his place.

He leaned back against a low wall beneath the windows. His arms were burning, the good burning of muscles put to good use. The room was filled with the vital heat of the fire he had built and lit, the fire that would save them all. A good heat, the kind that calms shivers and warms the chill from wet and tired bones. The fire felt good.

He closed his eyes and didn't try to stop the tears that seeped out between his eyelids, running in warm paths down his face. They ran down his cheeks and over his lips, which opened into a wide smile, tasting their saltiness. He laughed as the tears poured from his eyes.

Colin walked over and stood beside him. The giant rat still sat on his shoulder, sniffing at the smoky air.

"Why are you laughing like that?" he asked.

Jonathan laughed and sobbed and looked at the beautiful fire through the blur of his tears.

"Because I want to go home," he answered.

"Then why are you crying?"

Jonathan didn't wipe at the tears. He let them burn in his eyes until they were full and flooded out.

"Because I want to go home," he said. "Because I want to go home."

ACKNOWLEDGMENTS

As always, there are far too many people to thank and recognize. I feel so grateful and lucky to be surrounded, both professionally and personally, by so many many people who support, help, encourage, and inspire me.

My family, who cheers me on more than they probably ought to. Karen, Eva, Ella, Claire, Mom, Dad, Erin, Justin, Grandma, Noni, Bops, Brian, Linda, Michelle, and Michael. Love you all.

My friends, who lift me up but keep me grounded. Jabez, James, Carver, Andy, Tim, Kat, Jen, Pat, and Aubrey.

My agent, Pam Howell, and Bob DiForio, who always have my back.

My amazing editor, Nick, whose judgment and wisdom make all my stories better, and to all the tremendous folks at Scholastic: Jeffrey, David, Emily, Lizette, Reedy, Sheila Marie, and all the rest. I'm so over-the-top lucky to be with such an amazing team. And a special shout-out to Nina Goffi, the cover designer who has given my stories such beautiful faces to show to the world.

To the wonderful educators I'm so lucky to work with at Mission View Elementary and the Wenatchee School District. There are too many of you to name, but you are an inspiration and a force of incredible good in the world and I'm blessed to know you.

To all the fellow writers I've been fortunate to meet and connect with over the past couple years; it's been a thrill to get to know you, and the world is richer for having your stories. Your dedication to storytelling has inspired and strengthened my own.

To all the good folks at NaNoWriMo . . . *Scar Island* began as my first NaNo project several years ago, and look at it now! Thanks for supporting writers and writing, dreamers and dreaming, and a mad month of marvelous imaginings.